T0194700

GREG STALLWORTH

CROSS WIRES

CROSS WIRES

iUniverse books may be ordered through booksellers or by contacting:

iUniverse
1663 Liberty Drive
Bloomington, IN 47403
www.iuniverse.com
1-800-Authors (1-800-288-4677)

ISBN: 978-1-5320-8105-7 (sc)
ISBN: 978-1-5320-8108-8 (e)

Library of Congress Control Number: 2019912613

Print information available on the last page.

iUniverse rev. date: 08/28/2019

ACKNOWLEDGEMENTS

Cross Wires has been a dream come true for me as an Author. This has unmistakably been the most challenging literary work that I've ever written because of its extreme detail of a near real life story. With any project that's time consuming, you need the support of many during your journey of which I have gratefully received. I want to first thank God for giving me the gift of writing and patience to pursue my dream of becoming a successful Author. I would like to thank my wife Rose and my entire family for giving me the support, time and understanding in pursuit of my dream. Special thanks Stan Ross, Curtis Drake Shepard, David Livers, Shan'tel Renee Collins, Hazel Wimberly Wagner, Khrys Styles, Rebekah Richardson, Martha Bonham, Minnie Black and all my friends for your prayers and inspiration. I also want to thank the entire staff at the Public Library of Cincinnati and Hamilton County, Reading Branch where Cross Wires was written and developed, your support will always be remembered. Lastly, who would have thought a young boy from Lincoln Heights, Ohio (Zone 15) would grow up and live out his dream to become a successful recognized Author. Thank you! Enjoy the read!

PROLOGUE

Cross Wires brings to memory quote from the past that says "What Doesn't Kill Us, Only Makes Us Stronger. This dramatic thriller based in Miami, Florida brings to light in vile detail diverse scenes of love, trust, deceit, hate and deception, all in world of Corporate America. This suspenseful novel intensely brings to light the damaging pitfalls of working in Corporate America. A world where anyone can be subjective to financial greed, even to the point of risking their life. Written by Greg Stallworth, author of Double Deceived is unmistakably a story that will have you mystified to how one's life can change in the blink of an eye.

CHAPTER 1

Walking through the automatic doors of the Pyramid Office Tower in downtown Miami, Aaron Williams, a sharply dressed 35-year-old African American corporate executive hurriedly enters an open elevator. As the elevator ascends rapidly, Aaron brushes off the shoulders of his Brooks Brothers navy blue pinstripe suit while adjusting his cherry red tie that is sitting neatly on his pearl white dress shirt. As the elevator doors open Aaron exits toward the Remington Corporation office suites at the end of the hallway. Aaron walks into reception area where he is greeted by Camille, an attractive receptionist of Hispanic descent. "Good morning Mr. Williams," says Camille, a very attractive receptionist of Hispanic descent speaking in a soft and pleasant voice. "Good Morning Aaron?" says Camille smiling. "Good morning Camille," says Aaron smiling back as he walks toward his office. Entering his office Aaron places his briefcase on his oak colored executive desk. As he settles into executive chair Aaron immediately checks his phone message panel and realizes that he has received an interoffice call from Robert Remington Sr., the Chairman and CEO of the company. Aaron immediately presses the button to call and after several rings Mr. Remington answers. "Good morning Aaron, how are you? I would like to see you in my office to share some information with you," he says. Nervous and wondering what Mr. Remington might want to share with him, Aaron acknowledges his boss's request. "I will be right there sir" he says. Placing the receiver down Aaron slowly gets up from his chair and walks out of his office past the reception area. Enters the office suite Aaron walks past Kim Downing, the corporation's Financial Controller. Aaron greets Kim cheerfully but gets an unprofessional response from her. Giving Aaron a fake smile, Kim responds sarcastically. "I already know. I guess you can go in," she says. Aaron knocks on the open leading into Remington's office. Seeing Aaron at the door Remington responds. "Come on in Aaron. Close the door and have a seat please," he says. Aaron complies with Remington request and takes a seat directly in front of him. Allowing Aaron to get comfortable Remington began to speak. Aaron, I received a call from Fortune Magazine this morning informing me that my corporation made their Fortune 500 listing as one of the top five hundred companies that has grossed one hundred million dollars in the country. Aaron, we made the list due to your leadership in helping us secure that fifty-three million dollar contract with Cardinal Enterprises." "In all my years running this corporation this is a dream come true,' he says, standing up from his desk and shaking Aaron's hand firmly." "Thank you Mr. Remington for giving me the opportunity to succeed and grow in your corporation" says Aaron smiling radiantly. As an act of benevolence Remington reaches in his desk drawer and pulls out a white envelope and hands it over to Aaron. "Because you worked tirelessly day and night in securing that bid and with the national attention we've received I wanted to show my appreciation. I think you will appreciate the generous bonus I am giving you," says Remington. Shocked at Mr. Remington's generosity Aaron gets emotional realizing the benefits of his efforts and the honor that was bestowed on him. Aaron gets up from his chair, goes over and gives Mr. Remington a hug of appreciation. "Thank you, thank you Mr. Remington for this bonus! This is the best gift I've ever received in my life," he says as his voice starts to break up. Mr. Remington smiles as he responds. "Aaron you are very deserving of what you have received this morning. Please enjoy it," he says. Aaron leaves the office smiling as he walks past Kim who doesn't speak or acknowledge him while he exits.

Arriving back to his office Aaron immediately takes out his cell phone and calls his wife to share the good news. After several rings his Michelle answers the phone. "Hello," she says. "Hello!

"Hey baby, I have some great news to share. You're not going to believe it Michelle," says Aaron extremely excited. Anxious to hear what her husband wants to share Michelle moves the conversation along. "What is it honey?" she asks anxiously. Calming down before speaking Aaron continues. "This morning Mr. Remington called me into his office. I was thinking it had something to do with my employment. You know most times when Michelle when you're called in it's usually for something you done wrong," he says. Well he called me in to tell me that our corporation made the prestigious Fortune 500 list as one of the top financially successful companies in the country. Hold on! Hold on baby! That's not all! He told me the reason we made the list was that I got Cardinal Enterprises to sign that fifty-three million dollar contact." "Then after congratulating me he gave me an envelope with a bonus check of fifty thousand dollars.

Wow, I just received an email from Mr. Remington inviting us to join him and his wife for a weekend of celebration in New York City where his company will be at the Makers and Movers Foundation annual event," says Aaron. Hearing the great news, Michelle screams with joy over the phone. "Baby, that is awesome! I love you! I love you! I can't wait until you get home to give you a big hug and a kiss," she says becoming almost speechless. Maintaining his composure Aaron replies. "Honey, let's celebrate this special occasion by going to your favorite French restaurant at Harbor Point? I need you to get dressed for a night out on the town. I want you to wear that sexy dress that you know turns me on. You know that red satin mini. Let your hair down tonight baby because we're going to paint the town red, "says Aaron laughing. Michelle was quick to remind her husband about the last time she wore that dress when they went out for dinner. "Baby, remember when I wore that mini and men was looking at me lusting," she says laughing. Thinking back on his past behavior Aaron "I promise I won't get jealous like that again. I was very possessive of you. With age comes maturity," he says. Michelle laughs at her husband's reply. "Well, I hope so," she says. Aaron needing to change the subject replies. I will be home around six o'clock to pick you up for a romantic date says Aaron passionately.

Michelle, curious to what her husband will be wearing for the evening inquires. Honey, do you want me to select something nice out of your closet to wear this evening?" asks Michelle.

Responding to his wife's question Aaron responds immediately. "Michelle, I got that all covered.

Let me surprise you this evening with my fashionable attire. Trust me, I dress to impress just for you! I will see my beautiful sexy wife at six o'clock sharp okay?" Michelle responds romantically to her husband. "Okay I'll be ready when you get here baby. I love you," as they end their phone call.

After his romantic conversation with his wife Aaron immediately dials 411. After three rings a young lady answers the phone. "Hello, directory assistance may I help you?" the operator asks "Good Afternoon I would like the number to Prichard Limousine Service," says Aaron. "Just a moment please," the operator responds. After a brief wait the operator returns to speak with Aaron. Sir, the number is area code 305- 222-0000. Would you like me to connect you?" she asks. Aaron replies immediately. "Yes please." "Thank you for using directory assistance." she says pleasantly. After several rings a reservation specialist answers. "Good Afternoon Prichard Limousine Services, may I help you?" she asks. "Yes, my name is Aaron Williams and I would like to make a reservation for one of your luxury stretch limousines for this evening," says Aaron. After hearing Aaron's immediate need for a limousine the reservation specialist asks Aaron several questions regarding his reservation request. "Sir, how many will be in your company," she asks curiously. "Just me and my lovely wife, Aaron replies. The reservation specialist looks over her list of available limousines. "Well sir, based on the number in your party it sounds like you will only need one of our smaller limousines that seat four. Would that be okay?" she asks. Hearing her recommendations Aaron responds. "Sorry, this is a very special occasion so I will need one of your larger limousines you have available. You know like a Fortune 500 style limousine," says Aaron exhibiting a sense of humor. Not understanding what Aaron meant by that the reservationist replies. We don't have Fortune 500 limousines however we have one of our top of the line limousines available. It seats twelve comfortably complete with a wet bar and surround sound stereo system. The rate will be three hundred dollars an hour with a minimum three hours. That does not include gratuity. This luxury limo is usually reserved for celebrities, corporate leaders and dignitaries," says the reservationist. After hearing the rates and the type of people who normally reserve the limousine Aaron responds immediately. "Consider me a corporate executive and I want to reserve it for this evening," says Aaron. Going into her computer the reservationist brings up the limousine that Aaron is requesting. What is your method of payment Mr. Williams," she asks. "I will be paying with my American Express card. "What is your card number please?" "My number is 3471209982131156, shares Aaron. "and what is your expiration month and date," "My expiration date is May of 2022, and my three digit is 550," replies Aaron. After processing Aaron's card the reservationist responds. Mr. Williams where would you like to have our driver pick you up?" she asks. Aaron pulls out his itinerary for the evening he had written on a piece of paper out of his suit coat. The first pickup will be at the Pyramid Office Tower located at 224 Corporate Boulevard at 5:30 p.m. From there we will arrive to 35408 Cherry Blossom

Lane to pick up by beautiful wife. Then we will go to the Harbor Pointe revolving restaurant on the beach. Then we will end the night at the Lover's Suite downtown where the driver can take us where we will stay for the night. I have one other request. If you could have in the limousine a dozen white roses, a bottle of Regal Chablis wine, the one imported from France on ice with two heart shape wine glasses with some soft romantic music on your surround sound system," asks Aaron. As the reservationist types in the itinerary information into the computer she updates Aaron. "Mr. Williams, I have all your information regarding your itinerary to give to your chauffeur. His name is Phillip and he we will be there for your first pickup at five thirty. Is there anything else that I can help you with Mr. Williams?" "I think that we will be all," Aaron responds. "Thank you for choosing Prichard Limousine Services and have a wonderful evening" she says pleasantly before ending the call.

Understanding the short amount of time he has to prepare for his romantic evening with his wife, Aaron turns out the lights to his office leaving his office. Approaching the receptionist desk Aaron smiles at Camille before saying goodbye for the day. "Camille, I will be leaving for the rest of the day. If anyone needs to reach me I can be reached by cell phone. I'm going to take the afternoon to prepare for an evening dinner date with my beautiful wife. Have a great weekend Camille," he says smiling. Camille smiles back and poses a question for Aaron. "Aaron can you one day sit down with my husband and talk to him about the importance of taking his beautiful wife to dinner sometimes?" she says laughing. Aaron looks at Camille giving her a suggestion. "Why don't you surprise him by taking him out to dinner?

That will make him think twice to what a loving husband supposed to do for his beautiful wife. I will assure you it will not be a problem anymore," says Aaron assuredly. Camille stares at Aaron in disbelief how simple he made her issue resolvable. Aaron leaves the office and hurriedly makes his way to an open elevator and goes to the ground floor walking to the parking garage. Dropping the convertible top to his shiny black Mercedes sports car, Aaron takes the Airport Boulevard exit then makes a left into the parking lot of Vito's Italian Men's Wear. Aaron immediately goes in to be fitted for a designer suit to wear for the evening. Walking into Vito's he is greeted by the owner and tailor. "Hello sir. I'm Vito, how can I help you today?" says Vito, a medium build dark hair man with an Italian accent who smiles at Aaron. "Yes, I was looking for a white designer double breasted suit to wear this evening." Looking at Aaron's physique Vito responds. "How tall you and what are your measurements, your waist size and your suit size," he asks in his Italian ascent. "I am six foot one and I am a 36 in the waist 32 length and wear a size 42 in a suit coat," he tells the tailor. The tailor based on Aaron's measurements goes over to a specific rack and looks at a white double breasted white suit Aaron may be interested in wearing. Vito takes it off the rack and walks up to looks up Aaron smiling as he holds up the suit. "Bingo my brother, this suit is perfect for you, size 36 waist and 32 lengths with the coat size 42. You came to the right store. You got a good taste for classy suits. You seem like a playboy getting ready to pick up a sexy lady for the evening" says Vito smiling at Aaron. Aaron responds back immediately. "As a matter of fact I am but this sexy beautiful lady just happens to be my wife," says Aaron looks smiling at Vito. Vito looks at Aaron smiling, "I'm sorry my brother, no disrespect to you or your wife," he says apologetically. I just figured wearing threads like this you was going to have some beautiful company. Handing the suit to Aaron, Vito directs him over to the dressing room. "Why don't you go in there and try it on to make sure everything fits. By the way the last person who came in and bought a suit like that was a former NFL star player who went by the name Neon Deion. You heard of him haven't you? He was the star athlete that told the NFL team that was going to draft him out of college that in order for them to sign him for the money he wanted they would have to put him in layaway," says Vito laughing out loud. Aaron breaks out in a laugh himself as he goes into the dressing room to try on the suit. Moments later Aaron comes out of the dressing room wearing the designer suit smiling. It feels like this suit was made especially for me. I want it and I will be wearing it out of here," says Aaron. Today I was informed by my boss that the contract I secured with my company got us on the Fortune 500 listing as one of the most successful companies in America," says Aron glowingly. In fact the boss invited me and my wife to New York City this next weekend where he will be honored. But now I am taking my beautiful wife out this evening for dinner, dance and whatever comes next if you know what I mean," he says smiling. Vito hearing Aaron's success congratulates him. "That's awesome my brother! You mean someone in corporate America is giving credit to a black man for taking his company to success?" Excuse me my brother I hope you don't take this the wrong way. I'm an Italian brother and nobody has given me credit for shit for what I have done for others. I have suited some of the most famous celebrities and dignitaries in this country putting them in some of the finest Italian designer suits. I have dressed men who are on Wall Street, who have received awards at the Grammy, Emmy and other well-known events. I have dressed your first black President my brother," says Vito getting noticeably angry talking about his experiences. I want my reparations too dammit!" he says turning his anger into a smile. Aaron smiles at Vito as he poses in the mirror to see get a second look at how his suit fits. "I hear you man. It just happens that I got a boss who is of a different color from me who is very appreciative of my ability to make him a profit," says Aaron carrying the clothes he wore in the store. Vito responds laughing. "I tell you what brother when you get back to wherever you work, do me a favor. Find your boss, put him on ice and frame his ass. Why? Because you probably won't find many bosses like yours in corporate America. By the way, how does the suit feel?" Vito asks reassuring that Aaron is satisfied. "It fits perfectly. So perfect like I said that I'm going to wear it out of this store. Do you have a garment bag to put my other clothes in?" he asks. Sure, I'll be right back," says Vito as he goes behind the counter to retrieve a garment bag. After putting his clothes in the bag Aaron hands Vito his credit card to pay for his purchase. Before Vito goes to the register to ring up the purchase, he looks at Aaron. "My brother you need some accessories to bring out that suit. I recommend that you get a white silk shirt and lay a red silk tie on it along with a red handkerchief to put in your suit coat pocket. I also suggest you wear a pair of my cherry red leather shoes we got on sale. They're a perfect fit with that suit," says Vito directing Aaron over to the shoes and accessories area. After purchasing the shoes and accessories Aaron goes back to the register to check out. Vito looks at Aaron smiling. "Brother, if I had let you get out of here with only that suit you would have been in trouble. Now you're going to be the talk of the town with your lady on your arm. Have a great romantic evening my brother," says Vito. With his designer suit on Aaron thanks Vito and walks out of the store.

Getting in his car, Aaron speeds off to freeway back to the Pyramid Office Towers awaiting the limousine's arrival. Looking at his watch Aaron notices that it is already five o'clock walks from his car into the building. Aaron calls to check on Michelle before getting dressed making sure everything is fitting perfectly. Moments later he looks out of the window and see the white stretch limo waiting out front of the building. Realizing that they are early Aaron feels comfortable with his time. Aaron goes out to greet the chauffeur and shakes his hand. "I'm Aaron Williams. I'm ready to go pick up my Queen," says Aaron smiling radiantly. "Yes sir," says the Chauffeur as he graciously opens the door for Aaron allowing him to take a seat before closing the door gently. The Chauffeur leaves the office building heading to the freeway Aaron smiles anticipating their arrival to pick up Michelle.

Arriving at their home on Cherry Blossom Lane the stretch limousine slowly pulls up in the arch driveway. As the driver comes to a complete stop Aaron takes his cell phone out and calls his wife notifying her that he was home. "Hey baby, your prince charming is here waiting to receive you." As the driver gets out of the limo and opens Michelle, a slender woman with a honey brown complexion is seen coming out of the home looking gorgeous like a celebrity model. Wearing a cherry red satin mini dress with a plunging neckline, she reveals her cleavage and outline of her firm breast. She compliments her evening dress with a pair of black diamond teardrop earrings, a diamond studded necklace, off black designer stockings, cherry red clutch purse and red stilettos. Draped over her shoulders is a silk cape that enhances her elegant look. As Michelle walks toward the limousine she falls into the waiting arms of her husband. Her silky black shoulder length hair is glistening in the sun as it bounces in place with her every move. Aaron smiles while embracing his wife while giving her a kiss before assisting her into the limousine. As the chauffeur closes the door the feel of passion and romantic love over takes the limo. The Chauffeur slowly leaves the drive as Aaron and Michelle cozy up to each other. Realizing the mood the chauffeur turns up the music in the rear of the limo playing romantic music as he travels smoothly down the freeway. Aaron reaches on the shelf of the wet bar and grabs a bottle of Regal Chablis that was put on ice along with two of the heart shape wine glasses. Slowly pouring drinks in two glasses Aaron hands Michelle a glass then gives a toast. "To my lovely wife Michelle, may we continue to have a happy marriage and achieve financial success for as long as we live, cheers" They give each other a passionate kiss before taking a sip of their wine. Looking around in the limo Michelle notices rose petals scattered indicating Aaron's romantic affection for her. Michelle smiles romantically at her husband. "The last time you and I had rose petals in our presence was the night we made passionate love after we got married," she smiled looking at him romantically.

Moments later the limousine pulls up to the entrance

of the Harbor Pointe Revolving Restaurant, one of the finest five star restaurants in Miami. Aaron and Michelle get out of the limousine and is immediately greeted by the Concierge who welcomes to the Harbor pointe revolving restaurant. "Hello Monsieur and Mademoiselle. Under what name are we holding reservations for you this evening?" he asks politely. Aaron looks up smiling at the Concierge. "The reservations are under Aaron Williams," he says. Looking at the reservation list on his computer tablet the Concierge acknowledges the Aarons reservation and escorts them to an open elevator taking them to the revolving restaurant on the twelfth floor. As the elevator goes up to the floor, and opens, Aaron and Michelle is graciously greeted by the restaurant's Maître D who is informed by the concierge the name of the guests. Walking up to Aaron and Michelle the Maître D makes his formal greeting. "Hello Monsieur and Madame, welcome to the Harbor Pointe Revolving Restaurant. Please follow me to your seats," he says smiling at the couple. Following the Maître D to their table both Aaron and Michelle are extremely impressed with the romantic and soft ambience of the five-star restaurant. Arriving to their table located in a very romantic dimly lit area the Maître D seats Michelle. "Our waiter Pierre will be here to serve you shortly. Enjoy your dining experience," he says. While waiting for the waiter to arrive Aaron reaches inside his suit coat pocket and pulls out the envelope containing the fifty thousand dollar check and handing it to his wife. "This is for you baby. It's for you believing in me through all that we been through. Without you none of this could be achieved," says Aaron as he takes her hand romantically. As tears start trickle down from her eyes Michelle's is emotionally filled with joy as she looks at her husband. Aaron, I love you! It is an honor being married to you," he says. Moments later the waiter comes to the table and greets the couple. "Hello Madame and Monsieur, my name is Pierre and I will be your waiter for the evening. Can I start you off with something to drink," he says. Aaron looks a brief look at the wine menu and looks at the waiter. "Yes, we will like to have a bottle of your Regal Chablis on ice with two heart shaped glasses" says Aaron looking at Michelle romantically. The waiter smiles at the couple as he writes down their order. I will be right back with your Regal Chablis", says the waiter. As the waiter begins to leave the table Aaron interrupts him and curiously asks. "I made arrangements for a special surprise through management. I think something is missing?" says Aaron smiling. The waiter unsure to what Aaron was talking about smiles at Aaron. "I will check into immediately Monsieur," he says. Reaching over and gently holding his wife's hand Aaron whispers romantically. "I love you. Soon we're going to be so financially successful that anything you want I will be able to provide," he says. Moments later the waiter brings a dozen of white roses and a gift box wrapped in a bright red bow. Seeing this placed at her table, Michelle gets very emotional. Realizing that her husband has arranged this loving delivery she began to cry tears of joy. As the waiter leaves the table Aaron slowly unwraps the gift box and opens it up and pulls out an eighteen-karat diamond studded ring and gently places it on Michelle's ring finger. "Michelle, this is a show of my love and devotion to you," he says. I hope that you will cherish this moment for the rest of your life," he says as tears continue to stream down Michelle's face. Speechless, Michelle gives her husband a lengthy kiss ignoring the fact that other restaurant guest nearby are watching them. Approximately ten minutes after Aaron shard his fit with his wife the waiter arrives at the table with their drinks. "Monsieur and Madam, may I get you an appetizer to start off? Aaron looks over the menu then looks at his wife. "Do you want some appetizers? "No honey I already know what I want as an entrée" she says calmly. "I'll have the prime rib dinner with scallop potatoes, asparagus dipped in cream sauce and honey carrots. "What would you like Sir? I will have the same as my wife, Aaron replied. As the waiter writes enters their order on his tablet he leaves the table allowing the couple to have some more personal time. Aaron looks over to his wife. "Baby, we're not going home tonight. I've made reservations for us to have a romantic night at the Lover's Suites downtown," says he says smiling. Michelle reaches over giving her husband a kiss whispers to him. "Baby, the way you're making me feel this evening I promise I won't disappoint you romantically tonight when we get to the hotel," she says. After a night of dining under candlelight and viewing the beautiful downtown skyline from the revolving restaurant windows, the couple leaves the restaurant to their waiting limousine to the hotel.

CHAPTER 2

itting on the park bench drinking a bottle of wine Robert Remington Jr. and Rob's friend David, his alcoholic friend is having a conversation. Looking much disheveled Rob is arguing with David over who needed to buy the next bottle of wine. As their conversation continues and gets heated, David changes the subject to Rob's family. "Rob, I wish I were in your shoes. With all the money your old man has and his promising you the company after he retires how could you screwed that up by becoming a drunk," says David emphatically. Turning red and getting upset Rob stares at David after taking another drink from his bottle. Shut the hell up! You have no idea what I went through. He promised me the company after I graduated from college but he wanted me to kiss his ass begging him for money and treating me like a dog. He was always on me about who I associated with and my lifestyle. Then he turns around and hires this black guy as his Vice President of Operations. Then you ask me why I am an alcoholic! I hate the hell out of him," says Rob angrily. David shakes his head in shame staring at Rob. "You had it made Rob," he says. Rob looks at David. "What in the hell do you mean?" asks Rob. David stares at Rob surprised that he doesn't understand. "What I mean is getting in the condition you are in today. You could be on top of the world man," he says. Rob looks at David in dismay, "I think that's a bunch of crap. He always wanted others to think that he loved me but he hated me the day that I was born. If it wasn't for my mom I would probably have been dead," says Rob upset. David looks at Rob. "Man, I can hear your eulogy now. Robert Remington Jr. loving son of Sarah and Robert Remington Sr., owner of the Remington Corporation who died homeless from complications of a poor relationship with his daddy, depression, being a drunk and what he thought was reverse discrimination by his daddy. Why don't you get yourself sober, check into a rehab center and show your dad that you're ready to take over the company since he promised it to you," says David. Moments later David observes Rob's older sister coming up the walkway into the park. Spotting her brother sitting on the bench Deena walks closely toward him smiling. "I figured I would find you here Rob," she says openly. Robert looks over at his sister and starts to get very frustrated by her presence. "What do you want?" says Rob loudly. Deena takes a seat on the park bench next to her brother to bring bringing him some good family news. "Rob, I came to tell you that dad's company made this year's Fortune 500 list as one of the top in the country in financial earnings," says Deena very excitedly. Mom asks me to try to find you and invite you to the house for a celebration dinner at six o'clock in dad's honor Friday before they leave for New York to attend the awards presentation," says Deena. Rob stares at Deena giving her a critical look. "So I guess I'm supposed to be delighted and humble myself to that bastard huh?" says Rob angrily. Yeah I know how it goes. I come over to dinner to hear everything he has done for the company and the family only to get ridiculed by him," says Rob sarcastically. Deena, listening to Rob's verbal tirade of her dad responds angrily. "Don't blame mom or dad for your problems. They gave you everything you needed to succeed in life. They sent you to one of the best schools Harvard University where you got your degree. Rob, you chose your own path to destruction. If you were smart you would get yourself in a rehab program to deal with your alcoholism. After getting yourself sober maybe you can start talking to dad about giving you another chance to run his company. Rob, why did you waste your time going to college only to end up in the streets?" asks Deena demanding an answer. Rob immediately shouts out to Deena in response to her comments. "Oh blame me! Blame me for everything that went wrong in our family and in my life. How soon have you forgot the times when dad used to come home from work, drunk and beat the hell out of us for nothing? I guess that was my fault too huh? I guess it was my fault for him being an alcoholic? Now you wonder why I'm a drunk! Since his company is Fortune 500 I guess all those things will be forgotten huh? Well Deena it's not. He is a lying, abusive and cheating no good ..." Deena tired of Rob's verbal assault on her dad, interrupts his conversation. "I don't have to sit here and listen to you discredit our family, especially dad. It's about you Rob! You need to clean up your life before you start dirtying up others. By the way since you don't check up on mom anymore I thought I would let you know that mom went to the doctor on Wednesday and she found out that she has breast cancer. She has to go for a biopsy and additional test in the next few weeks. Rob you need to get yourself together, put your feelings aside and be there for mom. The family celebration starts at 7:00 p.m. Friday and mom wants you there" says Deena with a serious look on her face. Obviously upset Deena gets up from the bench and walks away without saying goodbye. Rob in a moment of sadness hearing of his mom being diagnosed with cancer places his face in the palm of his hands hiding the tears that are streaming down his face. David realizing Rob's emotional pain finding out his mom's illness remains silent out of respect of what he is going through. Rob gets up from the bench without saying a word or acknowledging David walks away stumbling through the park obviously intoxicated. Concerned about Rob's safety, David gets up and follows Rob in hope of providing support through his most difficult time. As David he gets closer to Rob he shouts out to him. "Rob, Rob! Let me talk to you! I know you are upset," says David. Rob immediately turns around and looks at David as tears continue to stream down his face. "David, shut the hell up! You have no idea what I'm going through right now. Leave me the hell alone!" says Rob as he walks hurriedly across the street stumbling almost getting hit by a vehicle as he goes into the neighborhood halfway house where he resides.

CHAPTER 3

Arriving at her parent's house Deena walks in calling for her mother to inform her of the news. "Mom, mom where are you?" shouts Deena. Sarah, hearing Deena from the laundry room responds loudly over the sound of the washer. "I'll be there in a minute." As Deena paces the floor waiting for her she reaches in the candy bowl and grabs a couple of mints and quickly puts them in her mouth. Moments later Sarah shows up in the living room and gives her daughter a hug. As she releases her embrace Sarah asks curiously. "What's going on Deena?" says Sarah. Deena walks her mom over to the sofa to sit her down before sharing the news of her speaking with her son Rob. "I saw Rob today and I told him about dad's company making the Fortune 500 list and unfortunately he was not impressed. He was blaming dad for everything that has went wrong in his life. Mom, he's not taking any responsibility for what's he has done to cause his problems. Not surprised at what Deena is saying Sarah stares at Deena curiously. "Did he say he was coming over for dinner this evening?" she asks. Deena looks at her mom and shakes her head solemnly. "I doubt it mom, the way he was talking about dad I think it would take a miracle for him to show up tomorrow," says Deena.

Sarah shakes her head in disappointment. "It's a shame that he feels that way Deena. We tried to give Rob everything he needed. I don't understand his bitterness toward his dad," says Sarah. As the conversation continues Sarah interrupts her visit with her daughter. "I'm sorry Deena, I have to finish up dinner before your dad gets home and the guest arrive, plus I have to get dressed," she says apologetically. Understanding mom's situation Deena immediately gets up from the sofa preparing to leave. "Mom, I need to leave and get dressed as well. I'll see you later," says Deena giving her mom a hug. As Deena walks she turns around and stares at her mom, "Minus a miracle I hope that Rob shows up for dinner. He needs his family and our love," says Deena confidently. Sarah, confused by her daughter's comment asks curiously. "What's wrong with Rob? What does he need? She asks nervously. Deena with a smirk look on her face responds. "Probably a better attitude, rehab and love from his family if you ask me," she says as she goes out the door. Looking out the bay windows watching Deena get into her car Sarah obviously still confused to what she meant shakes her head and goes to the kitchen to continue preparing dinner for the evening celebration.

The clock approaches six o'clock, family and guest start arriving at the Remington house for the celebration dinner. At the lengthy dining room table, family and guest start getting seated around the table. Mr. Remington takes his traditional seat at the head of the table. Deena and her husband along with her Uncle Stan and his wife are seated on each side of the table by Mr. Remington's Financial Controller Kim and her husband. As the family and guest are in conversation with each other, Sarah brings the final dish of food out of the kitchen and places it on the table before taking her seat at the end of the table opposite her husband. Mr. Remington looks around the table getting everyone's attention. "I guess everybody is here, can we start this evening off in prayer?" Sarah looks at her daughter Deena curious if Rob was going to show up for dinner. Sarah stares at her husband; "I guess you can start dear, she says in a low key voice. Mr. Remington pushes his chair closer to the table. "Please bow your heads. Dear Heavenly Father" … Suddenly Mr. Remington's prayer is interrupted by a loud knock at the front door. Obviously upset that he had to stop his prayer Remington sounds shouts out. "Who is it? With no immediate response Deena quickly gets out of her chair to see who is at the door. As she goes around the arc shaped entrance to the living room she observes Rob standing at the door appearing to be sober. Surprised to see Rob at the celebration, Deena smiles as she greets him. "Hello Rob, come on in! We've been waiting for you," she says giving him a hug. As Rob walks into the dining room he observes mom, dad, and family guest sitting around the table waiting to devour the entire delicious looking food in front of them on the table. He goes over and immediately gives his mom a big hug, kisses her on the cheek, and speaks to everyone else. "Hello, sorry I'm late," he says apologetically as he takes a seat next to his mom. Disturbed by his son's presence and interruption of his prayer he had started, Mr. Remington tries again. "May I try to have prayer again?" Dear Heavenly Father we come to you this evening asking that you bless us as we celebrate my company's success in the business world, and it's recognition as a Fortune 500 Company. As my wife and I along with my Vice President and his wife prepare for our trip to New York tomorrow for the awards ceremony, I ask that you make our trip a safe one for all involved. Last but not least Father, I ask that you allow individuals to get their lives in order so that they may not bring down the family name. I ask these and all things in your son Jesus name Amen."

"You may go ahead and eat," Rob Sr. says openly. Deena sneaks a look at her mom realizing that her dad purposely directed the end of the prayer toward Rob, and his lifestyle and problems with alcohol.

As the family and guests start preparing their plates, passing dishes to each other, Mr. Remington stares at Rob in disgust. Sarah, realizing the negative vibes generated by her husband toward her son attempts to initiate some positive interaction. "Junior, it's so good to see you! How have you been?" she asks. Rob looks at his mom smiling, "I've been surviving," he says. As he prepares his plate his dad speaks out across the table. "Decided to come out of the cold Rob? His dad says sarcastically. Sarah intervenes before Rob can respond. "Honey, please eat your food," she says pleading with her husband to be respectful at the dinner table. Looking at his wife Mr. Remington replies, "I was just welcoming him back home. Sarah attempting to be respectful, considering that they have family and guest in their presence replies. "All I'm saying dear is let's talk after dinner," she pleads. Seeing that his dad wants to create problems with him, Rob interrupts his mother. "Mom, let him talk. Dad, do you have something to say to me?" he asks staring him in the eye. Robert Sr. stares back at Rob in anger. "Hell yes I have something to say. In fact I have a lot to say. It's a shame that you have tarnished the image of this family by turning into a drunk. I had you all set up to take over the company after I retired. I sent you to college to get your business degree and what did you do? Wasted all my damn money and destroyed my dreams. Look at you, a damn bum," he says angrily. Rob, allowing his dad to go through his verbal tirade calmly gets up out of his seat pushing his plate away from him, causing tension among the family and guests. Rob, staring at his dad raises his voice across the table. "Yeah, you sent me to college to get my degree. You did all that for your own self-image. I destroyed your dreams huh? What about the dreams you destroyed, when you use to come home from work drunk and were physically abusive to Deena and I. Remember when you threatened that you would kill us if we told mom of your abuse? You talk about destroying your dreams. What about the way you destroyed mom's dreams, when she found out about Rodney? You know Rodney, the child you had outside your marriage that you hid from her by paying child support under the table to keep it quiet. That arrangement worked until little Rodney became a teenager and tried to extort money from you. Realizing that he was going to go public, then, and only then was when you confessed your sins to your wife. What a poor example of a father. All the while you were giving your colleagues and friends the impression that you were in a so-called happy marriage. You are nothing but a good for nothing-old ass infidel. Yeah I'm telling all of your business, or as you would call it letting the skeletons out of the closet. Now I'm asking you, is that a dream or a reality?" Robert Sr. gets up in a fury, and walks quickly over toward Rob and confronts him. "Don't you ever talk to me like that," he says screaming at Rob. Without any provocation, Robert Sr. slaps Rob in the face. "Get the hell out of my house you no good bum," he says angrily. As Rob takes a step back from the effect of the physical assault, he walks toward the door. Looking back at his dad he angrily replies. "Yeah dad, the truth hurts don't it, Mr. Fortune 500? I hope your colleagues and friends don't find out that the real Robert Remington Sr. is a devil hiding behind his successful company, dressed in his Brooks Brothers suits. As Rob goes out, slamming the door behind him, the family and guest are in a state of shock of what they had just heard, and their reaction to it. As Mr. Remington goes back to his seat, he apologizes for the outburst between him and his son. He asked everyone seated at the table to continue to enjoy the meal that his wife so gracefully has prepared.

CHAPTER 4

Arriving at the Miami International Airport, Aaron and Michelle carry their carryon baggage to Concourse A where they are scheduled to meet the Remington's for their scheduled 10:45 A.M. flight to New York City. Arriving at the airport concourse, Aaron spots the Remington's at the will call section of the ticket window. Directing his wife to follow him Aaron walks up near the line. "Good Morning Mr. and Mrs. Remington," Aaron says in his most pleasant greeting. Turning around and seeing Aaron and his wife, Mr. Remington smiles. "Well Good Morning Aaron and Michelle. Are you ready to enjoy the most fabulous event in the world?" Aaron smiles at Mr. Remington radiantly. "We are most honored to accompany you and your wife to this event," he says. Getting the tickets and checking in their luggage, Mr. Remington urges his wife along with Aaron and Michelle to follow him to the Concourse security checkpoint. After going through a thorough search by airport security, the couples are allowed to enter the tunnel leading to the entrance of their commercial flight.

The couple settles into their seats as the turbo engines revved up preparing for takeoff to their destination,

New York City. Upon take off, the stewardess walks pass passengers smiling making sure that they have their seat belts on. After a video recording regarding flight safety and a greeting from the pilot, commercial flight 4409 takes off. After two hours of non-stop flight, the plane circles and eventually lands at La Guardia International Airport making a loud noise as it eases it's speed leading up to the unloading ramp.

Getting their carry on out of the luggage compartment above, Aaron and Michelle along with Mr. Remington and his wife exits the plane. As the couples are walking through the Concourse, Michelle looks at Sarah smiling. "Sarah, don't we have two of the most awesome men in the world? "Yes we do, but it took a lot of our feminine persuasion to help them get where they are," says Sarah laughing humorously. Taking the escalator down to the baggage claims area, Aaron and Robert Sr. identify and take their luggage off the baggage carousel and join their wives to board a taxi to the Hilton Hotel. Entering the lavish and spacious hotel, both couples approach the registration desk to check in for a weekend of fun and excitement. Once registration is completed the bellhop takes their luggage to bring to the room. After arriving to their room, Aaron takes a sigh of relief as he looks out over the downtown skyline from his fourteen floor hotel room. "New York City, New York City, the town that doesn't sleep," he says smiling at his wife. Michelle, smiling at Aaron responds. "Baby, you earned this beautiful experience and I'm so proud of you," she says holding his hand.

After a romantic evening of sightseeing through the streets of New York City and Times Square, viewing landmarks, and listening to a gifted musician share his talents on the street corner sidewalk, Aaron and Michelle stop for dinner. Entering an Italian restaurant called D'Amico Aaron and Michelle are cordially seated in this casual restaurant. Moments later a waitress comes to the table. "Hello my name is Cindy. Can I start you off with something to drink?" Aaron politely looks at his wife waiting for her to respond. "Yes, I would like a glass of sweet iced tea with lemon," she says. "I'll have the same he says. Aaron. The waitress scribbles their order on her pad, and proceeds to tell them what the special is for the day. "I will give you time if you need to look over the menu," she says. Aaron and Michelle knowing what they want respond. "We want a large pizza with Italian sausage with pepperoni," Aaron says smiling at the waitress as she acknowledges their order and leaves the table.

After enjoying a very delicious dinner in a very intimate dining atmosphere they pay their bill and casually exit the restaurant. Checking out the various entertainment values Aaron and Michelle head back to the hotel stopping to take pictures of the neon glowing establishments. Once back at the hotel Aaron and Michelle head to the elevator that takes them to the floor of their hotel room for a relaxing and romantic evening with each other.

At daybreak the telephone rings several times startling Aaron who was in a deep sleep, tired from his active day. Reaching over to the nightstand to pick up the receiver he answers. "Hello," Aaron answers in a hoarse voice. "Good Morning Aaron. I was calling to invite you and your wife to breakfast. What time can I expect you at the restaurant?" Aaron looks over at his wife who was awakened by the call.

"We can be ready in an hour," says Aaron yawning. "Great, we will meet you in the restaurant downstairs," says Mr. Remington. Before getting out of bed, Aaron reaches over and puts his arm around his wife's shoulder and smiles at her. "Baby, this has been a great week for us, hasn't it? First it was the Fortune 500 listing then the receiving the bonus check and now the trip here to New York City. We have been blessed," he says smiling. Michelle smiles back at her husband. "Let's just make sure that we stay humble through it all because we know that none of this would be possible without God," she says. Looking at the clock on the stand Michelle looks at her husband. "We better get up and get ready so we can be on time," she tells Aaron as she pulls the comforter off her body.

After getting dressed, Aaron and Michelle leave their hotel room and head towards the elevator down the hallway. Arriving in the hotel lobby they stop at the registration desk to get information about restaurant locations. Receiving information about the location of Melton's Restaurant where they're scheduled to meet the Remington's for breakfast. As they enter into this lavish eatery with glowing lights and pictures of historic landmarks around New York City. As they walk in Aaron immediately see the Remington's at a table for four. Showing the waiter that their company is already seated they are escorted to the table. Mr. Remington noticing the couple approaching gets up from his seat to greet the Williams. "Good Morning, please have a seat and join us," he says smiling. "Good Morning to both of you," says Aaron smiling. Moments later after Aaron and Michelle gets settled in the seats the waiter arrives at the table. It looks like everyone is here. Are you ready to order?" Mr.

Remington stares at the waiter. My wife and I would like to have your steak and egg combo with a bowl of fresh strawberries, two slices of wheat bread and two large glasses of orange juice," says Mr. Remington. "How would you like your eggs and steaks sir?" asks the waiter. "We would like our eggs sunny side up and our steaks medium well please," says Robert. The waiter looks over at Aaron and Michelle. "What will you like to order?" he asks smiling. Michelle looks up at the waiter after viewing the menu. I will have the steak and egg combo as well with a bowl of fresh pineapples, a large glass of cranberry juice and a cup of regular coffee," she says smiling back. "How would you like your steak and eggs?" Michelle responds openly. "I would like to have my eggs scrambled light and my steak well done please," she says. The waiter then looks at Aaron. And what would you like to have sir?" he asks. Aaron smiles as he looks at Michelle. "I would like to have exactly what my beautiful wife ordered," says Aaron, The waiter smiles as he responds. "Now, that it love. That was easy" he says laughing as he writes down their order and he leaves the table to place their order. Michelle looks at Sarah smiling and curious. "I must ask Sarah, how was it that your husband knew exactly what you wanted for breakfast without asking you?" Sarah laughs and smiles at Michelle. "If you were married for 44 years like we have been you would think he would know by now," says Sarah looking at her husband smiling and nudging him. Michelle looks at Aaron sarcastically. "I hope Aaron doesn't get to know me that well," she says smiling and planting a kiss on her husband's cheek. As the couples continue their conversation and humor the waiter arrives to the table with their breakfast. After placing their meals and drinks on the table the waiter ask if there was anything else he could get for them. Seeing everyone nod that they were okay the waiter responds. "Enjoy your breakfast," he says as he walks away. Aaron asks everyone at the table if he could say a prayer before they dine and with everyone's approval said a prayer that concluded with a Amen. Aaron while preparing to eat his breakfast looks over at his boss smiling. How does it feel this morning knowing that you received one of the nation's most coveted recognitions being one of the top 500 businesses in the country financially?" he asks. Mr. Remington glances over at his wife and responds. "Well, it's a great feeling knowing that the hard work of many that has brought me success with my company. It starts with the best person in the world who happens to be my wife. Then it continues with the best employee I have ever hired who happens to be you Aaron," says Mr. Remington beaming. "So to totally answer your question it was a teamwork effort. When we get back they will be interviewing us about our success, "he says smiling.

After eating a delicious breakfast and another day of sightseeing Aaron and Michelle decided to come back to the hotel, rest up before going to a gala on Times Square. After four hours of rest and two hours of Michelle prepping they prepare for the spectacular event. As they leave their hotel room for the reception prior to the gala, Aaron puts on his black designer tuxedo with matching shiny leather shoes coupled with a white ruffled shirt with burgundy cummerbund and bow tie. Michelle dressed in a jet-black satin designer evening gown with a slit on the right side shows her sexy figure. She compliments her gown with matching black high heels stilettos accompanied with diamond studded matching teardrop earrings and a black clutch purse.

Entering a waiting taxi outside the Hilton Hotel Aaron and Michelle is taken to Times Square for all the festivities. Aaron and Michelle upon arriving enter the gala ballroom for a reception with a host of dignitaries who have gathered to meet and socialize. After two hours of socializing and drinking they leave the reception to their reserved seats where Mr. Remington and his wife greet them. "Hello," says Mr. Remington. As invited guest begin to flow into the ballroom and take their seats, Winston Millhouse President of the Makers and Movers Foundation comes to the podium to speak. "Good Evening guest and dignitaries, welcome to the Annual Makers and Movers Awards Ceremony. We want to get started by acknowledging our newest and first time recipient of the Makers and Movers award recipient, the Remington Corporation from Miami, Florida. The Remington Corporation is a major public relations and marketing firm located in Miami earned over five hundred million dollars during the year 2017. The tremendous success of this company has placed them on the Fortune 500 list at 498. I'm happy to introduce to you the Chairman and CEO of the Remington Corporation. Mr. Robert Remington Sr. Please welcome to stage Robert Remington," says Winston Millhouse. Mr. Remington gets up from his seat; receiving congratulatory hugs form his wife, Aaron and Michelle. As Mr. Remington walks up to the podium to a thunderous applause from the audience, he acknowledges them by waving in appreciation. Steadying himself at the podium Mr. Remington addresses the audience. "Hello, first I would like to thank the Makers and Movers Foundation for this prestigious acknowledgement. As all of you are aware, no company or corporation can achieve success without a successful team. I say that because our inclusion into such an exclusive foundation such as the Makers and Movers Foundation had a lot to do with my Vice President. Mr. Aaron Williams who is with me this evening is the primary reason that we are here. Mr. Williams was able to secure major contracts that took us over one hundred million dollars in gross earnings. He is the heart and soul of our operation. I would like to bring to the podium our company's hero, Mr. Aaron Williams. Can you give him a round of applause?" Aaron smiling with joy gets up from his seat, receives congratulatory hugs from his wife and Mrs. Remington before joining Mr. Remington at the podium. Aaron, before reaching the podium gives Mr. Remington a handshake. Aaron, taking a brief moment to regain his composure speaks. "Thank You, Thank You for the acknowledgment you gave me. First, I want to thank God for giving me the gift of salesmanship. I also want to thank the Makers and Movers Foundation for identifying our corporation and its achievements. And just as importantly, I want to thank Mr. Robert Remington Sr. the Chairman and CEO of the Remington Corporation for giving me the opportunity utilizing my skill set to secure the contracts needed for us to reach this milestone as a corporation. He hired me, believed in me, an African American executive when other companies refused to give me a chance. Because of that I will be forever grateful. Thank You," says Aaron stepping away from the podium and going back to his table to another round of applause and the continuous flickering of lights from cameras in his face.

After the banquet and awards presentation the Remington's and William's make their way through a sea of guest out into the lobby area where individuals were giving each other congratulations and farewell wishes before leaving the hotel. As Aaron and Michelle was moving away from the crowd attempting to go to the elevators and back to their rooms, a group of reporters from various media outlets surround him wanting interviews. With cameras clicking and the flashes of cameras in his face Aaron politely attempts to answer some of the reporter's questions. Mr. Williams' how does it feel to be the first African American executive to work for the Remington Corporation and achieve the status you have?" asks a reporter from a major television media outlet. Aaron overwhelmed at the attention that he is receiving responds. "It feels great not only as an African American, but a person who has been through so much to get where I am. I am so blessed," he says. Moments later another reporter asks "Mr. Williams how are your co-workers going to handle all the attention that you are receiving, after being championed for you being the reason that your company is receiving this award?" Aaron smiles at the reporter and replies candidly. I thought Mr. Remington made that very clear in his acceptance speech. Didn't you hear it?" he asks staring at the reporter. Knowing that it is getting late and his wife is getting weary from all of the day's activities, Aaron responds to the reporters. "I will take one more question please," smiling as he speaks. "Mr. Williams I am a local reporter from Miami covering this story where the company is located. I remember doing a story with Mr. Remington Sr. where he had said that his son, Robert Jr. would be his successor when he retired. My question is in two parts. Where is Robert Jr.? My second question is how that will affect your position, if what he said becomes a reality?" the reporter asks. Catching Aaron off guard with such sensitive questions, he replies nonchalantly. "I think that's a question that you would have to ask Mr. Remington. I am not in position to respond to that. Thanks for your questions. The wife is getting tired and we need to rest up for tomorrow," he says. As he attempts to get away from the barrage of questions that reporters continue to ask him, Mr. Remington looks over from afar the activity around Aaron and smiles before getting into the elevator with his wife.

CHAPTER 5

Arriving at the Care Unit Treatment Center Rob realizes that his drinking has become so serious to the extent where he needed to be admitted into alcohol rehab facility. As he enters the facility and walks up to the information desk he is greeted by the information specialist. "Good morning! May I help you?" she asks. Rob looking very stressed and irritated stares at the female specialist. "I'm here to sign myself in to dry out" he says boldly. "What is your name please, "the specialist asks causing Rob respond immediately. "My name is Robert Remington Jr. but not like my dad" he says angrily. Shocked at Rob's response the specialist looks at her admissions sheet. Not seeing Rob's name on the list she looks up at Rob and replies "Sir, I don't see you on the admissions list. Were you referred here at the treatment center?'" she asks curiously. Rob stares at the specialist, gets upset and raises his voice. "No! Didn't you hear me say that, I said I wanted to sign myself in to get dried out?" putting the specialist on alarm of his behavior. Pushing the chair back making sure she has accessibility to the security radio if needed, the specialist calmly tries to explain the admission procedures. "Sir, I'm sorry but you can only be admitted to the Care Unit if you were referred by your physician or treated into the emergency room and admitted. Rob, listening to the specialist comments about admission to the facility gets upset. He immediately starts pacing the floor then all of a sudden violently starts kicking furniture and knocking magazines off the table as he rants profanity. The specialist realizes that Rob is close to getting physically aggressive picks up her radio and calls CU security. "Security to CU main lobby, stat! Security to CU we have a male subject white male who is being very unruly and destroying property. Please come stat" As the specialist puts down her radio, she gives Rob his space in hopes that he calms down before security arrives. "Sir, I have someone coming down to assist you," she says in a calming voice. Rob walks up on the specialist screaming. "I don't want to see no damn person, I told you I need help," he says angrily. Suddenly three hospital security officers show up in the lobby observing Rob going into what they believe is an emotional meltdown. Cautiously approaching him the security officers surrounds him to avoid any continued aggressive behavior. Rob feeling crowded by security screams at the officers. "Either admit me or I'm going to kill myself," he says staring at the officers about to go crazy. Based on Rob's threats of suicide and his attempts to leave the area the security supervisor immediately ordered that Rob be physically restrained while a call was being made to the Mobile Police Department. Moments later the police arrive to the scene. After a detail discussion of Rob's volatile behavior and the threat suicide the life squad unit was called to transport him to University Hospital Emergency for treatment.

Arriving at University Hospital Emergency, Rob is met by hospital security as the ambulance pulls up at the entrance.

Waiting inside the sliding doors are the Psychiatric Nurse and intake staff as the security team assist in transporting Rob from the ambulance into the emergency room. The nurse, observing the behavior instructs the officers to bring him who is on a stretcher into the evaluation room to transfer him to a hospital stretcher and switch restraints. After reviewing the incident report then allowing time for him to get settled into the room the nurse goes to begin her triage. "Hello Mr. Remington, my name is Cynthia. I am the nurse here today. Can you tell me what is going on today?" she says in a pleasant voice. Rob looks up at the nurse appearing calmer than in the previous hours. "I have a drinking problem and I need some help," Rob says openly. "I promised my mom that I would go get help for my drinking problem. I went to the Care Unit Center to get help and they couldn't help me. So I had to tell them that I was going to kill myself just to get help. So that's why I am here. The nurse curious of his drinking problem emotional problems inquires. "So Rob do you feel suicidal?" He looks at her smiling. "No, I don't feel suicidal, but I feel that I'm going to die if I don't get help for my alcohol problem" Probing more before writing her notes and consulting with the Psychiatrist that is on call the nurse stares at Rob curious. "Robert, how long have you been drinking," she says preparing to take notes on her tablet. Rob, struggling to adjust to the physical restraints tries to explain his history with alcohol. "I've been drinking wine heavily since my dad lied to me five years ago after promising me that would take over his company when he retires, "he says. Curious to what he alluding to the nurse probes with more questions. "What does your dad have to do with your drinking problem?" she asks inquisitively. "Well, when he lied to me and hired this black guy I became depressed and started to drink to deal with my pain," Rob says angrily. Typing in her notes while pondering her thoughts the nurse looks up at Rob. "So going back to your thoughts of suicide did you have a plan? "asks the nurse. Rob getting upset with the series of questions the nurse is asking him gets very quiet in an act of defiance So I'm hearing that you're willing to get help for your alcohol abuse problem, right?" she asks. Rob responds immediately. Yes, that's what I was trying to do before they brought me to this dungeon," he said sarcastically.

The nurse gets up from her chair, close her tablet and began to walk away. "Rob, I will be back. I need to talk to the social worker and the doctor, okay" Rob nods affirmatively still struggling with the restraints he was placed in when he arrived. Going into the consultation room the nurse sits down with the social worker and the resident psychiatrist on duty to explain her conversation with the patient during her triage. "Robert Remington Jr. is a thirty year old Caucasian male whose chief complaint is alcohol dependency. Arrived to PES via the police as a violent mental demanding to be admitted at the Care Unit and then threatening suicide. Patient denies feeling suicidal. He states that he mentioned suicide in order to get admitted to the Care Unit. When he was denied admission, he became very volatile and started pacing in the lobby, kicking furniture causing a disturbance which led to the police being called. After being transported to Psychiatric Emergency Services patient states that he has been drinking wine every day for the last five years. Patient blames his dad for his alcohol problems, stating that his dad lied to him about taking over the company that he owns.

He made reference to dad hiring a black guy in his position. According to the patient his bad relationship with his dad is what led him to continue his abuse. Patient is very much disheveled and smells of alcohol which leads me to believe that he'd been drinking before arriving to the Care Unit. His vital were stable but blood pressure was a little elevated," the nurse said clearly. The doctor after reviewing Rob's medical chart gets up out of his chair to see Rob as part of his psychiatric evaluation. Entering the observation room the doctor introduces himself to Rob. "Hello Mr. Remington, my name is Dr. Norris. I want to take a few minutes to talk to you," says Dr. Norris. Rob raises his head up to get a clearer view of the doctor. "No offense doc but can you just call me Rob? I hate that last name," he says angrily. "No problem Rob. The nurse informed me why you're here and some of the issues you are having so I won't burden you with that. However, I need to ask you some more questions. How many meals do you eat a day?" Rob stares at the doctor. "I eat once a day," he replies. Curious why Rob isn't eating more inquires. "Why aren't you eating more on a daily basis?" doctor asks. Rob responds sarcastically. "Because the halfway house I stay only serves meals two times a day and I don't eat that slop they serve for breakfast. They put us out at nine o'clock in the morning and we are on our own until dinner time. Dr. Norris shaking his head makes his notes from Rob's conversation with him. "Are you having any stomach pains throughout the day? Not so much hunger pains but sharp pains?" the doctor asks Rob. "Hell yeah!" says Rob. They have me so bent over at times, I feel like I'm going to die" he says rubbing his stomach where the pain hurts. The doctor feels the area and notices an unusual lump below his bellybutton that is a cause of concern. "Now I want you to take several deep breaths while I feel where you are experiencing the pain. As Rob takes several deep breaths the doctor continues to examine Rob just relax I'll be back, I need to talk to the nurse," he says calmly walking back in the consultation room. Once getting back to the room Dr. Norris summons the nurse to call the floor and have Robert Remington admitted to 8 WEST with a diagnosis of depression with manic episodes of suicidal ideation caused by alcoholism. "I want the patient to also have a medical consult for severe gastrointestinal infection and a workup to rule out any early stages of cirrhosis of the liver. Forty minutes later, Rob was informed that he will be admitted to the hospital and taken to his room on 8WEST.

CHAPTER 6

Entering the high rise office building where the Remington Corporation is located Aaron is surprised to see a crowd of local media reporters outside the corporate office. Not realizing they were there to interview him for achieving the Remington Corporation's first Fortune 500 Award. Attempting to avoid the media blitz Aaron tries to walk through the stream of reporters and cameras but is stopped by reporters seeking to interview him. After continuous request to be interviewed Aaron takes honor their request. "Mr. Williams, Matt Lynch from Channel 4 News. I heard you were responsible for getting the Remington Corporation the Fortune 500 award. Can you speak on it?" asks the reporter. "Yes, I was able to secure a major bid from a local company that placed us on the Fortune 500 list but it wouldn't have been possible without the leadership of the owner Mr. Remington" says Aaron, smiling at the reporter. "Michael Young of Channel 7 News, Mr. Williams I heard you were the only African American working with the Remington Corporation. How do you feel about a company that has a history of not being diverse as it relates to hiring minorities?" he asks seeking an immediate response from Aaron. "Well I have been here at the

Remington Corporation for six years and I haven't had or seen any problems as it relates to race. I think it is just a matter of time before those numbers change as it relates to hiring more minorities if they are qualified" says Aaron smiling. Watching the gathering of reporters from her office window, Kimberly immediately gets upset and storms out of her office and goes into Remington's office slamming the door behind her. Mr. Remington looks up surprised at Kim's antics and stares at her. "What in the hell is going on Kim?" asks Remington demanding an answer. Kim leans over Remington's office desk literally screaming at him in anger. "What the hell are you doing about Aaron?" shouts Kim. Confused to what she is talking about Remington stares at Kim giving her a disturbing look. "What are you talking about?" he asks trying to stay calm. "Robert, what in the hell am I supposed to do with all the local media in the hallway blocking the entrance to your business interviewing Aaron about what he did to get your corporation to Fortune 500 status? Why are you allowing Aaron to have all these interviews? Why are you just sitting back in your office letting Aaron get all of the attention for something you should be getting the credit for? You built this business from the ground up to where it is today. Shouldn't they be interviewing you as the owner of the Remington Corporation? What do you have to say about this entire media blitz that's going on? I'm not able to do my work because of all the noise outside of my office. In fact you promised your son that when you retired that he would take over the corporation. It's unfortunate that you don't even have a relationship with your own flesh and blood. Have you ever thought about the reason why your son is having problems? Have you ever thought that your son turned to alcohol because he had a void in his life? Robert did you ever consider your son's feelings or point of view? How do you think he felt when he found out that you hired a black man to the position that was promised to him? Now look at what is happening now! A black man who is now trying to take over your company? Aaron getting all of this attention for the Fortune 500 award your corporation received is a damn shame! Oh by the way, I fail to mention that Aaron is receiving a lot of phone calls and messages since his recognition. I suggest that you check his phone calls and voice mails. I believe he is masterminding a takeover of your corporation. Don't lose every damn thing you worked for Robert!" says Kim as she leaves angrily out of her boss' office. Sitting at his desk in shock at Kim's comments against Aaron, Remington stares out of his bay window looking over the downtown skyscraper. Moments later Remington calls Kim back into his office to share a few words with her. Kim comes into the office still angry takes a seat and stares at her boss waiting to hear what he has to say. "Kim, I need to tell you this and I will not say it to you again. Aaron is an employee of high character and there is no reason for me to believe that he will attempt to take over my corporation. In fact I see him as a person who has brought value to my business operation as a professional. And yes, he is the reason why we reached Fortune 500 status. That's all I have to say to you. As far as I am concerned this will be our last conversation about what you feel Aaron is attempting to do to my corporation. Good bye" says Mr. Remington allowing Kim excuse herself from his office. Obviously disappointed with his decision Kim gives Mr.

Remington a sinister smile before exiting his office. An hour later Mr. Remington gets his paperwork as he prepares to leave his office for an out of town business meeting over the weekend. Realizing that Mr. Remington will be out of town on business Kim plots a plan behind his back to bring in a rogue technician to illegally cross the telephone wires in Aaron's office where she will receive his phone calls and voice mails. As Mr. Remington leaves his office and goes to the elevator Kim immediately goes into her phone directory to find the number of Ralph Lowell, a close friend who knows of a rogue technician who previously worked in telecommunications as an installer. Getting up from her desk and locking her office door for privacy she calls Ralph. "Good Afternoon Ralph, this is Kim. I need a favor from you. You know that young man that who formerly worked in telecommunications that you introduced me several years ago? I think we need his services here at the Remington Corporation" says Kim. After hearing Kim's request Ralph responds. "What's going on at Remington, "asks Ralph curious to what is going on. Kim responds immediately expressing her anger. We have an African American name Aaron Williams who is trying to take over the Remington Corporation and I am not going to let this shit happen. Robert is saying how good of guy he is. He is getting all the attention and lately he is getting a lot of phone calls here with some prominent people in this city. I believe he is trying to take over the corporation. I need to know who he is talking to so we can bring him down" says Kim angrily. After hearing Kim very upset Ralph responds. "His name is David. How soon do you need him Kim? He's only a phone call away" says Ralph. Kim anxiously replies "Well I need him this weekend to do the job" responds Kim hoping he is available. "Let me give David him a call Kim. I will call you as soon as I hear from him" says Ralph. Thirty minutes later Ralph calls Kim to inform her that he has arrange a meeting with her and David at six o'clock at Mario's Italian Restaurant on Main Street this evening. "That's great! I will be there!" says Kim thanking Ralph as she hangs up her phone displaying a cunning smile as he pushes herself away from her desk and leans back in her chair gazing at the ceiling pondering the next move. Later that evening Kim seen at Mario's Italian Restaurant, a small speak easy restaurant establishment known for providing businessmen to dine and make deals. Sitting in the dimly lit corner table of the restaurant, Kim looks out the window anxiously waiting for David to arrive. Moments later a Caucasian man around forty years old walks into the restaurant looking around suspiciously. Feeling that he is the one she is supposed to be meeting raises her hand like a prostitute flags down a potential customer directing him to her table. Recognizing the hand signal David comes back to the corner table where Kim greets him. "Hello David I'm Kim, Ralph referred you to me". "Have a seat," she says smiling. As David sits down Kim pulls her chair closer to the table to have more privacy. Would you like to have a drink? Everything is on me" says Kim smiling at him. David somewhat modest but needing an alcohol beverage takes Kim up on her offer. "I'll take a Long Island Ice Tea please with little ice," he says grinning. Immediately Kim calls the waiter over to take their drink orders. "We would like two Long Island Ice Tea double shots of everything with little ice. As the waiter takes their orders and goes back to the bar to request their drinks Kim speaking softly so no one can hear their conversation tells David her request. "David, I remember meeting you several years ago at the party for Ralph. When we met you told me you were in telecommunications and if I needed your services to call. Well, I need your services now! And I'll take care of you financially," says Kim smiling at David. David stares at Kim and responds. "What job do you want me to do," he asks curiously. Kim continuing to speak softly to avoid anyone hearing her responds. "We have a problem with an employee at the office that we need to resolve. We think he is undermining the company and we need to get to the bottom of it. I need for you to do cross some telephone wires between offices so we can find out who he is calling and who is calling into the office speaking to him and leaving voicemails. Can you make it happen?" pleads Kim. Looking at Kim smiling David responds. I can make it happen, however it may take me a couple of hours because there is a lot involved" says David seriously. Kim looks around the restaurant making sure no one is listening in on his conversation. "Can you make it happen this weekend?" she asks. "I can make anything happen if the price is right," he says confidently. Stopping the conversation after observing the waiter coming back to the table with the drinks Kim pauses. As the waiter places the drinks on the table, Kim gives the waiter her credit card. "You can go ahead bring us the bill" says Kim smiling at the waiter. As the waiter leaves Kim reaches inside her purse and pulls out an envelope with money in it. "I'll pay you twenty five hundred now. And twenty five hundred when after you complete the job," says Kim. David opens the envelope and looks at the cash money smiles and responds. "Deal, I can be there Saturday morning at ten" Kim hands David a piece of paper with the address of the Remington Corporation office address and replies. "I will meet you at my office around ten o'clock Saturday morning," she says smiling. After shaking hands David and Kim get out of their chairs and walks toward the exit. "I will see you then" David says as he leaves the restaurant and crosses the street. The following morning Kim is in her office looking out the window waiting for the technician David to show up to do the cross the wiring from Aaron's office to her office. As it becomes close to ten o'clock Kim hear the opening of the elevator in the hallway. She anxiously goes to the door and notices David getting off the elevator and greets him. "Good morning David! Glad to see you. Come on in and I will show you where everything is located. As David adjusts his tool belt he is shown the communication room at the end of the hallway. Needing to know which offices will be affected by the wiring of the phones David is taken to Aaron and Kim's offices. After getting the serial numbers off the phones David goes back to the communication room where there is a mass of wiring and starts using his pen light needle scanner to make sure the lines are active. Once he realize they are David begins to splice and add additional wiring to Aaron's and Kim's phone lines to have Aaron's calls and voicemails to be transmitted Kim's phone. Sealing the telephone wires with a plastic coating, David goes to Kim's office to add a device to her phone to activate the calls. Going over to Kim David smiles and looks at Kim. "The job is done. You should be able to receive all of his calls and voicemails. After receiving the good news Kim reaches in her pocket and hands David a folded envelope containing the twenty five hundred owed after completion thanking him for his service. "David, you're a life saver or should I say a company saver," she says smiling. "What you did today should avoid any illegal activities going on in this company by this employee who is attempting to take over the company" says Kim confidently. As Kim walks David to the elevator she thanks him again for his service. After seeing David leave Kim walks back to the office displaying a cunning smile attempting to do all she can to destroy Aaron's career.

CHAPTER 7

Bright and early Monday morning Aaron arrives to work happy to see the absence of the media who crowded the lobby on Monday. Walking past the reception desk he greets Camille in his usual manner. "Good Morning Camille, have I received any calls this morning?" Camille looks at Aaron with a tired expression on her face. "Are you kidding me? I've only been here an hour and before I could get situated I received four calls I sent to your voice mail," she says. "Since you have become famous your phone has been ringing off the hook," says Camille laughing. Walking to his office unlocking the door, Aaron sits his briefcase down and reaches over to his phone to check his voice messages that were sent to him by Camille. Anxious to listen to his voice mails, Aaron presses his telephone keypad to listen to his messages. "You have fourteen messages. To hear your messages please press one." Aaron presses his keyboard. "First message received Monday 6:10 a.m. from an undisclosed number. "I got that shipment of keys from Mexico that you wanted. Give me a call," says the first voice message that leaves Aaron confused to what the caller is talking about. Not sure of what is going on

Aaron pushes the button on his phone to hear the next voice message. "We're going to need a place to stack that money. What about that local banker friend of yours? Call me," says the caller. Shocked and confused at the voice message sent by the same person and not knowing what's going on nervously pauses and thinks what he is going to do with what he just heard. Not understanding the words keys and unsure what is means by stacking money he ponders for a moment who could he call to find out what those terminologies mean. Thinking they are street terms Aaron decides to call a longtime friend who is now in the streets. Feeling the need to keep his conversation confidential he gets up and locks his office door. Sitting down feeling nervous he calls his friend Lamont to see if he has any understanding regarding those words. Nervously waiting for Lamont to answer his cell phone Aaron paces the floor. "Hello, L speaking, who you," asks Lamont not recognizing the caller's number. "Lamont, this is Aaron how are you, he asks nervously. "I'm good Aaron, what's up with you? I know the stock market is down and you lost a lot of money and you need a loan from a loan shark huh," says Lamont laughing. "That's the only reason why you would be calling a broke brother like me. We don't even live in the same zip code, what's up," he asks. Aaron nervously responds. "Lamont I have a question or two. I received a call two voice mail messages at work and I don't understand words that were used in the messages," says Aaron. "I thought I would call you to see if you ever heard of them," he says. "Well Aaron I guess the words you don't understand must be from the streets not from corporate. That's the only reason you are calling me brother," laughs Aaron. Tell me what the voice messages says and I will do my best do decode them," says Lamont. "Well the first voice message said something about a shipment of keys from Mexico and the second voice message about finding a place to stack money, said Aaron nervously. "Brother, are you at work? It sounds like somebody is running a serious drug trafficking operation there. A key is short term for kilogram which means weight of drugs. Stacking money means getting lots money illegally usually from selling drugs and finding a place to hide it using the company as a front," says Lamont. You don't want to be tied up in that bullshit Aaron. It has to be somebody who has access to money and can funnel money in and out of the company. When it said the keys were shipped from Mexico that's fed shit if they're caught. And if they're stacking money like I said hiding drug money all kinds of shit comes with that like buying guns for protection and killings. I'm not telling you to be a snitch but it's on your phone and they go down you can be implicated because you knew about it. You could do some fed time which is straight time brother," says Lamont. Aaron, nervous about what Lamont shared about an illegal drug operation going on at the Remington Corporation and him being implicated made him extremely nervous. After getting off the phone, Aaron gets up from his chair and paces around his office confused to who may be involved and what to do. Realizing that the pressures of this situation are too difficult to maintain his sanity at work, he decides to leave work early. Feeling that going home ill was better than telling his boss what was going, not knowing if he was involved in a possible drug operation. Immediately grabbing his briefcase and turning his lights out, Aaron walks into the reception and stops at Camille's desk. "Camille, I'm going home for the day. I'm not feeling well" says Aaron nervously. Camille realizing that Aaron has only been in the office for an hour is curious to what is wrong. "Aaron what's wrong? You seemed okay when you came in this morning?" Aaron avoiding direct eye contact responds. I just think it's a virus. I'll probably be okay tomorrow. Please let Mr. Remington know that I left early because I wasn't feeling well. I'll talk to you later," says Aaron hurriedly leaving the office to the elevator.

Aaron arrives home surprising his wife as he walks into the family room where she is reading a novel. Surprised by his presence, Michelle closes her book and gives him a hug realizing something is wrong. "Baby, what's wrong," she asks continuing to hold him. Noticing the look in his eyes Michelle takes him over to the sofa to let him get comfortable. "What happen at work baby," she asks staring at him in support. Why are you home so early? Is everything okay," she asks. Aaron pauses and takes a deep breath. "Well things are not really. I got to work and after greeting Camille I went into my office to check my voice messages and that's where the trouble began," he said. Michelle immediately responds curious to what trouble he was talking about. Reaching out and holding her husband's hand she inquires. "What's the problem Aaron?" she asks pressing him on the subject. "Michelle, the man I thought was a very good and honest man may be a criminal," he says dropping his head in shame as tears start streaming down his face. Michelle shocked at Aaron's comments but still unsure what criminal activity he was referring to regarding his boss replies nervously. "What happened, "she asks. "I think Mr. Remington is dealing drugs in the company. "When I arrived at the office Camille informed me that I had a voice mails sent to my phone. I went into my office and checked my voice messages as I normally do before starting my day. When I retrieved several of my messages it was confusing. The first message was about a shipment of keys coming from Mexico and the second message said about needing a place to stack money and where to hide it. It mentioned about a bank," says Aaron nervously. When I heard those messages I got scared baby. I felt sick to my stomach and unsafe. I didn't know what to do at that moment so I decided to come home. I didn't want to talk t Mr. Remington, especially if he is involved. I have no idea why I was receiving these voice messages. I had no idea what those words meant in slang terms so I called my friend Lamont. You know he's a street guy and I figured he would know what they meant. And when I shared with him the voice messages he told me that those words were referring to drug activity. He went on to say that the word keys meant kilogram and it refers to the weight of drugs." says Aaron. He said stacking money meant making a lot of money illegally like the sale of drugs," says Aaron. Shocked over Aaron's revelation of his recent disclosure Michelle stares at Aaron. "So what are you going to do now you know of this information Aaron" she asks. "I don't know Michelle. How do I report this to the police? I don't know how much influence Mr. Remington has over the local police" says Aaron confused. Michelle pauses and puts her hand on her husband's shoulder for comfort. "Baby, how do you not report the suspicion of criminal activity once you know about it? What if the police find out that you have been withholding illegal criminal information? They can either charge you with obstruction of justice or tampering with evidence if you tried to hide or erase it" says Michelle sternly causing Aaron to look at the situation more critically. Aaron immediately gets up and nervously paces the family room floor confused of what to do with his dilemma. "Michelle I don't know what to do! What should I do?" says Aaron. Michelle gets up and takes her husband's hands and stands in front of him being sympathetic to his concern. "I think we should go talk to Pastor Wright for prayer and understanding. He always been the person we went to when we were dealing with issues that we were struggling with," she says. Aaron gives his wife a hug for her understanding of his plight and responds. "You're right. Let me him a call to see if he is available today" he says. Aaron pulls out his cell phone and calls Pastor Wright. After several rings Pastor Wright answers in a pleasant greeting. "Hello, Pastor Edmund Wright, may I help you" he says in his deep voice. "Hello Pastor Wright this is Aaron Williams how are you? Pastor Wright replies. "How are you and your wife" he asks. Aaron pauses attempting to respond to Pastor Wright's question and the reason he is calling. "My wife and I are doing okay but we need your consultation on something we are dealing with today. Is it possible that Michelle and I could come over and speak with you," asks Aaron. The Pastor sensing that Aaron and Michelle needed his immediate attention responds quickly. "Sure Aaron, I am available in the next hour. Just call me when you arrive" says Pastor Wright. Talk to both of you then" he says. Happy that the Pastor can meet with them, Aaron looks at his wife and smiles. Realizing what her husband is going through Michelle responds. "You know God has got us through many storms during our marriage. He will surely get us through this one baby. We just have to believe that God will get us through this one too, says Michelle spiritually.

CHAPTER 8

Getting off the elevator exhausted after a busy weekend Kim slowly opens her office door and takes a seat at her desk. She looks at her phone and realizes that she hasn't received any voicemail messages directed to Aaron's office. However looking at the control center she notices that Aaron has received quite a few voicemail messages this morning. Wow!" says Kim "It appears that our new celebrity is getting a lot of attention this morning" she says. Let me check on who is calling him" says Kim ease dropping on Aaron's voicemails. Pressing the device that David connected to her phone to listen to Aaron's phone messages she realizes that her messages are going to Aaron's office. Kim shocked and feeling extremely nervous that the voicemail that was intended for her were mistakenly sent to Aaron's phone. Curious to what other messages Aaron has received Kim presses the device again and realizes that messages about her drug involvement were also sent to his phone. Kim becoming concerned about Aaron's whereabouts goes into the reception area to speak to Camille. "Camille has Aaron been here this morning?" she asks anxiously. "Aaron was here but he went home ill about an hour after he arrived" says Camille. Curious to what Aaron's suspected illness is

Kim probes Camille for more information. "Did he say what was wrong with him," asks Kim suspecting he may have heard the voicemails and fake an illness. Camille, feeling she is being put in a situation hesitates before responding. "He said that he might have the 24 hour virus that's going around," replies Camille hoping that her response would be sufficient for Kim. Kim pauses then smiles at Camille. "Camille what time are you taking your lunch break?" she asks curiously. "I'll be going to lunch in five minutes. Do you need me to stay around?" she asks. "Oh no Camille, you go and enjoy your lunch. I was only asking to make sure we didn't go at the same time. I just want to make sure someone is in the office," she replies. Immediately after Camille leaves for lunch Kim looks around the offices to make sure no one was in the nearby offices. She goes into her office and locks the door and places a call on her cell phone. "Ralph speaking," Kim screams into the phone. Ralph, where is that son of a bitch you sent me who screwed up my phone lines," asks Kim. Ralph trying to calm Kim down informs her that David had just left saying that you didn't finish paying him the rest of the money for the job, he says. "Call him now and tell him that he needs to get his ass back over here and put my wires back like they were today! He screwed our phone system up where my calls are going elsewhere," says Kim angrily. Ralph realizing the seriousness of what has happened reassures Kim that he will get in touch with him. Kim, extremely nervous to what Aaron knows of the drug operation demands Ralph to call his contact person that he knows that will does murder for hire. After getting Ralph's promise that he will have a guy name Joe call her she hangs up on him in anger. As Kim ponders the worst case scenario that Aaron now knows about her involvement in major cocaine drug trafficking operation and the Remington Corporation her cell phone rings. "Joe speaking, what's up?" "Hey Joe this is Kim. You were referred to me by Ralph," she says. Joe takes a pause and then responds. "Yeah, he told me you would be calling. Let me take one guess, somebody rolled you for some money now you want him dead, right?" Kim replies immediately. "No Joe, I got an employee that I want you to take out immediately. Can we meet at Mario's in a half hour," she asks. "Yeah I can meet you there. "Cash only," he says laughing. "I will see you in a half hour," says Kim hanging up on Joe. As Camille returns from lunch Kim prepares to leave the office. "I will be gone the rest of the day Camille. I got a business meeting appointment," she says without hesitation. As Kim leaves the office on her way downtown to meet with Joe she notices a text message on her phone from Mr. Remington. Nervous to what he was texting her about she pulls over in a parking area to read his text. After reading the text notifying her that he would not be in the office for the rest of the week brought her instant relief and eased her fears. What you charging now days" she asks. Joe needing more information probes Kim further on the situation. "What happened?" Kim not wanting to take a lot of time of the phone presses Joe for what he charges. "We can talk about that later I need to know what you charge, she asks anxiously. "I charge five thousand when the job is done, says Joe. I got this black guy who is Remington's top assistant and he has gotten too much information on my drug operation. Not only is he trying to take over he got some voicemail messages about my undercover drug operation here at the Remington Corporation. This employee is going underground on me trying to take over the company. I hired the son of a bitch who supposed to be a top-notch technician in telecommunications but he screwed up my telephone wires. Instead of having calls come to my office, my calls went to this son of a bitch office. He crossed all my wires up. His name is Aaron and now he knows all that is going on with the drug cartel. He must go," says Kim. Hearing the story Joe agrees with Kim. You're right he must be taken out immediately. When do you want to do it" asks Joe. Kim ponders for a moment. "Let's make it happen Monday morning at seven forty five. That's the time he arrives in the parking garage to park. He is a tall muscular black man and he will be wearing a business suit. He parks in parking space 418 which is reserved. The space is not far from the parking garage exit where you can make a clean get away to the freeway," says Kim realizing that her plan will work. Realizing that he will be in a public facility, Joe understands that he will need to bring his silencer. Joe agrees with the plan but is waiting for Kim to talk about money. "Kim you're forgetting about what it takes to make this happen. I need to know about the money," says good looking at her very serious. "How much you're charging me to do the job," asked Kim curiously. Joe laughs for a moment. "Kim, let me put it this way Kim, we're the only profession in the world that doesn't get into that inflation bullshit. I'm not like gas and food prices and prostitution. My price stays the same to do a hit. Five thousand when I get the job done or your life if you don't pay me," he says in a no nonsense tone of voice causing Kim to respond immediately. "You won't have to worry about getting paid Joe. It will be worth it in the long run," says Kim smiling. By the way, did you hear that I got screwed by that rogue technician that Ralph sent me to cross the wires? He really caused me some serious problems. That is why I need you to put a end to all my problems, says Kim angrily. Joe smiles then respond. "Well Kim that's what you get when you hire an amateur to do a professional job. That won't be the problem here," says Joe. Meet me here Monday evening at six o'clock to pick up your cash," Kim says smiling as she shakes Joe's hand in agreement as they prepare to leave the restaurant. "That a deal, see you then" says Joe confidently.

CHAPTER 9

rriving at the office of Pastor Vincent Wright, Aaron presses the buzzer. Pastor Wright opens the door inviting Aaron and Michelle into his office. As they enter the office, he embraces both Aaron and Michelle. Come in and have a seat. Aaron and Michelle sit opposite Pastor Wright. Pastor Wright looks at Aaron, and said that he was concern by the tone of his voice, realizing that something was disturbing and upsetting him. Before we get started, let us stand join hands, bow our heads and repeat The Lord's Prayer: *Our Father, which art in heaven, Hallowed be thy name, Thy kingdom come, thy will be done, On earth as it is in heaven, Give us this day, our daily bread and forgive us our trespasses, as we forgive those who trespass against us, and lead us not into temptation, but deliver us from evil, For thine is the kingdom, and the power, and the glory, forever, and Amen!* Aaron looks nervously at Michelle, clears his throat before sharing his situation. "Well Pastor, I went to work this morning as I normally do greeting the receptionist and asking if I received any calls. She informed me that I had received about fourteen calls that were sent to my voice mail which is unusual for a Monday morning. As I sat at my desk, I activated my messages. After activating the voice mail, I heard two messages that implicated Mr. Remington of being involved in the distribution of drugs, more specifically cocaine that's coming into our city. I went to the next message and a man who on the voicemail said he had the Vice President of the bank hide some drug money into a series of money market accounts. I am thinking they were attempting to leave a message for Mr. Remington. I was scared and undecided as to what I should I do. Should I call the police or just ignore it. Pastor the reason why I'm struggling with my decision is just last week Michelle and I went to New York City with the Remington's to receive the prestigious award for making the Fortune 500 list. In addition, Mr. Remington gave me a bonus check for fifty thousand dollars for me securing the bids that got us the reward. Pastor Wright pauses to reflect back on some of the things that Aaron shared as he looked at Aaron and Michelle. Sitting up his chair closer to them Pastor Wright asks if they hold hands with each other. "Aaron and Michelle, I don't know how much I can assist you emotionally with your current situation but I can sure give you my opinion from a spiritual prospective. You are going through a storm. First, trust in God that he will deliver you out of this sinful situation. Remember, this battle is not yours. Speaking as your Pastor my advisement is truth. You must speak truth over power. You cannot partake in a series of corruption with the enemy even though they're giving you opportunities you never had before. You must do what's right in the eyes of God. You must eradicate out sin even in the workplace. I suggest that you notify the authorities immediately. Imagine, anytime that justice it not served, innocent people are victimized. I can guarantee you that if we don't report this illegal activity within 48 hours somebody possibly will be murdered on our streets. They can be killed because of a drug deal gone bad, drug overdose or territorial control. We read about it every day in this city. I have a friend that works for the DEA. I can call and let her know what's going on. I also recommend that you not go to work because of the implications that the investigation may cause you in the workplace. Are you willing to speak truth to power Aaron?" says Pastor Wright. Aaron confers briefly with Michelle before deciding on what they will do. "Pastor we are willing to speak truth to power. We are ready to go talk to the authorities," he said. Forming a circle of love by taking each other's hands, Pastor Wright says a prayer. "Heavenly Father, as we leave out on our journey of truth I ask that you protect us from the enemy. Allow us to speak with righteousness and love in the deliverance of your word. These things we ask in your son Jesus name. Amen! Aaron and Michelle, before we leave I would like to leave a scripture and words of encouragement. I would like for the two of you to meditate on Jeremiah 29:11 which says "For I know the plans, I have for you," declares the Lord, "plans to prosper you and not harm you, plans to give you hope and a future.""" God has a plan for you, just keep believing. You are facing obstacles in your life. I want you to trust and lean on God, He never fails, and with you trusting him, he can do the impossible. I've been pastoring for twenty three years, and I have seen him do it. God can turn this situation into an awesome miracle. The miracle I just spoke about, who's more capable than preforming miracles than God. Believe me son; I have seen God do it. Just think about what I have said. If you need to talk to me Aaron, I will be available for you. Stay encouraged Aaron and Michelle. Just wait on God to step in." Aaron and Michelle were so moved by Pastor Wright's words, that both had tears in their eyes. Aaron looks at Michelle, and he just held her. Pastor Wright handed both of them tissue, he embraced the both of them, and said "stay prayerful." I will meet you at the car," he says walking them to the door.

Arriving at the DEA station, Pastor Wright, Aaron and Michelle walks into the building and is greeted by DEA personnel. "Hello, my name is Pastor Vincent Wright and I'm here with Aaron and Michelle Williams. We would like to speak to Agent Asia Colburn please says Pastor Wright. She is aware that we are coming. The agent picks up the phone and calls Asia Colburn's office. Several minutes later a slender African American woman comes to the lobby and greets Pastor Wright, Aaron and Michelle. "Hello, Pastor Wright, how are you" as she shakes his hand. Pastor Wright introduces Aaron and Michelle to Agent Colburn. After a former greeting, Agent Colburn escort Pastor Wright, Aaron and Michelle to her office. After being seated Pastor Wright opens up the conversation with Agent Colburn. "The Williams came to me as their pastor, seeking advice on a serious problem that they are having. I would like for Aaron to share with you, what's going on," says Pastor Wright. "Agent Colburn, I'm the Vice President of Operations at the Remington Corporation that's located in the Pyramid Office Tower downtown. This morning I went to my office and after greeting the receptionist I asked if I had received any messages. She informed me that I had fourteen messages on my voice mail before I arrived. I went into my office to retrieve my messages and what I heard was alarming. The messages that I received I believe was for Mr. Remington, the President and CEO. The first message was from a man who mentioned that a shipment of drugs was arriving this morning and asked where he wanted the drugs distributed," says Aaron stuttering as he spoke. The Agent Colburn starts typing on her laptop information that Aaron was sharing. She looks at Aaron between typing the notes. "Did you save the messages you heard," asks Agent Colburn?" "Yes I did. There was another message that I heard," says Aaron. Inquisitive about the other message Agent Colburn questions Aaron further. "What did the other message say" Agent Colburn asks the agent. It said that this person at a bank was getting a bank staff to place the money into a series of money market accounts.

Aaron, you have any idea why those voice mails were coming to your office phone?" Aaron shakes his head and responds "as he take a few minutes to jot down notes as Agent Colburn began to wrap up her interview. "I will turn this over to my supervisor who will do the investigation. I will ask that while we are doing our investigating that you do not share information with any of your co-workers. It could seriously interfere with the investigation," said Agent Colburn emphatically. Collectively Aaron, Pastor Wright and Michelle nod in agreement with the Agent's request. Shaking their hands the Agent walks them to the door reassuring their follow up and investigation. After going to the Drug Enforcement Administration and sharing the same information with an agent, Aaron and Michelle thank Pastor Wright for his support, prayers along with accompanying them to the authorities.

CHAPTER 10

I t's 7:30 a.m. on Monday and Joe is sitting quietly in the Centennial Underground Garage adjusting the sights and silencer on his semi-automatic high-powered rifle. His burgundy Honda Civic is angled toward the exit accessible to the freeway for a clean getaway. Having a garage access card given to him by Kim, Joe mapped out his plan to avoid surveillance cameras by covering up his license plates with black plastic making it almost impossible to detect the letters and numbers on his plates when he leaves the garage. Having everything planned Joe relaxes while smoking a cigarette waiting for Aaron to arrive in his parking space. As seven forty five shows up on his watch Joe anxiously expects Aaron to be pulling up soon. As fifteen minutes elapses Joe gets very concerned based on what Kim shared about his scheduled arrival. Watching every car that comes on the level of the garage, Joe pulls out another cigarette out of his pocket anxiously awaiting the time to come so he can do his job. As a half hour passes and there is no sign of Aaron Joe gets irritated. Unbeknownst to Joe, Aaron was told by the regional drug enforcement agency and local law enforcement to stay home based on a tip they received which sabotages Kim's murder for hire plan. Upset he hasn't been able to reach Kim causes even more increased anxiety. Then after his final attempt Joe finally reaches Kim informing her that Aaron did not show up this morning at the parking garage. Kim realizing the seriousness of her plan happening today comes up with another scheme to have Aaron assassinated. She gives Joe Aaron's home telephone number to tell him that his sister was in a serious car accident and that he needed to get to the hospital immediately. When he shows up at the emergency room parking lot then he can take him out. Joe, upset that the original plan fell through agrees with the new plan because he needed the money. "Kim, you got me working overtime so this going to mean more money to do this job," says Joe sternly and without hesitation. "I will have your damn money. Don't sweat it. Just do your job," says Kim anxiously.

As Kim and Joe was plotting Aaron's death six armed federal drug enforcement agents all wearing blue suits shows up at the Remington Corporation offices armed with search warrants. Four men and two women agents stood at the door as one of the agents knocked loudly making their presence known. "Drug Enforcement Agents, stay where you are! We have a search warrant to search the offices," says one of the agents causing Camille to get extremely nervous and scared. Sitting at her reception desk by herself Camille is in a state of shock to what is happening. "What's going on," she asks shaking nervously. An agent walks up to her desk showing Camille the federal search warrant signed by a Judge to search the offices of Robert Remington Sr. and Aaron Williams. As Camille points into the direction of Mr. Remington and Mr. William's offices, the agents walks in that direction armed evidence bags and carriers to confiscates the computers, office phones and terminals out of both offices. While the agents are searching the offices Camille calls Mr. Remington waiting for him to answer his cell phone. "Morning Camille," Mr. Remington answers calmly. Camille, who is in a state of panic whispers through the phone to her boss. "Mr. Remington, there are six drug enforcement agents here with search warrants searching you and Aaron's office. Can you get here as soon as possible? I'm scared," Camille says continuing to look up trying to watch the agents' every movement Hearing Camille's frantic call Mr. Remington attempts to calm her down. "Settle down Camille I'm on my way, I am walking into the building as we speak," he says. Moments later Mr. Remington walks into his corporate office doors and is approached by one of the federal enforcement agents. "Are you Robert Remington Sr.," asked the agent. Moments after acknowledging his identity, the agent reaches to his side and gets his handcuffs to place on Mr. Remington. "Mr. Remington, we have a warrant for your arrest. I'm placing you under physical arrest. You have been charged with federal drug trafficking of a schedule 1controlled substance," says the agent. You have the right to remain silent and anything you say can and will be used against you in a court of law. You have the right to speak to an attorney and to have an attorney present during any questioning. If you cannot afford a lawyer one will be provided for you at government's expense," says the agent. Becoming very upset Mr. Remington shouts at the agent. "What in the hell are you talking about?" he asks. "I never sold drugs in my life! Why would I ruin my reputation or my company?" he asks. "I want to speak to my attorney now!" Remington demands. The arresting agent contacts the local police to transport Remington to the county detention center for processing while the assigned Judge on call considers a bond for his possible release. After a thorough search of both offices that took thirty minutes agents executing the search warrant leave the premises with evidence confiscated that included two computers, two office phones and terminals from the Remington Corporation. Shortly after the agents leave the premises amongst the local media who were informed of the arrest of Mr. Remington and the subsequent search served at the Remington Corporation. Upon coming into the building Kim witnessed the crowd of media and bystanders surrounding Pyramid Tower Office Building entrance. Wondering what was happening, Kim squeezes around the crowd to the elevators to the office to settle in and find out why is there such a circus atmosphere on the street. Walking into the offices Kim is greeted by Camille who is looking very despondent and upset. Kim walks up to Camille curious to why she is looking so sad. Camille Informed Kim that six drug enforcement agents with search warrants had just left and Mr. Remington was arrested for drug trafficking," says Camille staring at Kim crying. Kim, becoming very nervous knowing that he is responsible for all that had happened paces the floor before responding back to Camille. "Camille, you said they had a search warrant. What did they take from our offices," Kim asks curiously in hopes that what the agents confiscated won't expose her involvement in the suspected drug operation. Camille still visibly upset and crying responds to Kim's question. "They took the computers from Mr. Remington and Mr. William's offices and their desk phones and terminals. Those are the only offices they had search warrants to seize property. Somewhat happy to hear that her office was raided Kim immediately goes to her office to make sure nothing was disturb including her property.

CHAPTER 11

By midday the breaking news of Mr. Remington's federal indictments began to hit the airwaves through television, radio and print media. The community is shocked of the charges levied against this icon businessman. The conversation of Mr. Remington's arrest for drug trafficking among residents in the community was the talk of the town. Sitting at home in their family room Aaron and Michelle were watching television when the program they were watching was interrupted by breaking news of the federal indictments charges against Robert Remington Sr. Charges of drug trafficking, money laundering and extortion were mentioned in the news story. Visibly nervous and very upset Aaron immediately picks up his cell phone and calls Pastor Wright whom he relies on for advice and support. Aaron, realizing that he will be called as a witness to testify against Mr. Remington gets very emotional. Unable to reach Pastor Wright, Aaron places his phone on the table and places his head in his hands then takes a sigh of distress. "Why is this happening? Why?" asks Aaron. Why are these things happening to me?" Aaron asks slowing looking up at Michelle. Michelle looks at her husband sternly speaking in a soft tone. "Aaron, you know things happen for a reason. I think it's sending us a clear message that regardless of how good things appear to be, if there is any wrong doing it will be revealed in time. Mr. Remington has a good heart as far as being benevolent. Do you think he would do anything like that, "ask Michelle.

Moments later, the doorbell rings that startles both Aaron and Michelle. Aaron gets up from his chair and goes to the door to see whom it may be. Raising his voice Aaron inquires. "Who is it," he asks. "We're agents from the Drug Enforcement Administration with the Miami Police Department." Upon hearing the identification Aaron slowly opens the door. "Good afternoon, come on in," says Aaron nervous to what is going on. Showing their identification before entering the house, the agents and investigator follow Aaron to his family room as he introduces them to his wife Michelle before offering them a seat. Taking a seat and pulling out notes one of the agents from DEA informs Aaron and his wife Michelle of a serious situation involving Aaron. "Mr. Williams as you probably have heard, Mr. Robert Remington Sr. was indicted on various federal charges. As we continue our investigation we have confirmed information that a murder for hire plot was set up to have you assassinated yesterday. The murder plot was foiled when you didn't show up for work causing the suspected hit man to be unsuccessful in carrying out his mission. Aaron we're here to offer you protection until we complete our investigation and bring everyone involved in this crime to justice," he says seriously. Aaron, panicking immediately gets out of his chair asking questions to the agent. "Do you know who was plotting to kill me, "the Chief Investigator asks. "Mr. Williams, we have our suspicions based on our continuing investigation but we are not at liberty to share it at this time," he says staring at Aaron. Aaron pacing nervously around the room stops and asks another question. "When should I go back to work?" The agent from the DEA looks at him then at Michelle. My recommendation is that you do not go back to work until we take all the individuals into custody that are involved in this murder plot. The MPD will be doing surveillance around your house throughout the day and night. Until we can link those involved in this plot and arrest them we feel your life is still in jeopardy. We strongly recommend that you stay at home until you hear from us. If you see any suspicion or unusual activity around the area call police immediately," says the Investigator. Agreeing to the agent's request Aaron assures them that he will stay home until notified by the authorities. As the agents and Investigator leaves their home Aaron and Michelle become fragile emotionally. Hugging each other and crying Michelle is confused as to why someone would want to kill her husband. Going around the house making sure that all doors and windows are locked, Michelle comes back into the family room. Hearing the phone ringing Michelle goes over to answer. "Hello," says Michelle politely. There is a short pause between her greetings before the caller responds. "Is Aaron there?" says the caller speaking in a husky voice that Michelle could not identify. "No he is not here. May I ask whose calling?" The caller appearing to be getting irritated of Michelle's response muffles his voice. "I am a friend of Aaron's sister. Tell Aaron that his sister was in a serious car accident and he needs to get to University Hospital right away," says the caller before hanging up the phone. Shouting for her husband, Michelle frantically informs Aaron of the call. "Aaron you just received a call that your sister was in a serious accident and you need to go over to University Hospital. Reacting to the emergency about his sister being injured Aaron goes and gets his car keys and starts toward the door. Michelle goes over and blocks the door causing Aaron to get upset. "Michelle, what are you doing? I got to go," he says angrily. Pleading with her husband Michelle physically pushes him back away from the door. "Aaron, I think this is a set up to get you over there to kill you," says Michelle. Why don't you call Regina on her cell phone," she says hastily. Aaron, still upset with Michelle from leaving calls Regina's cell phone and gets no answer. Walking back to the door Aaron begins to physically push Michelle out of the way. "Michelle, get out of my way!" Michelle screams at Aaron upset. "Call the police! Call the police! Have them come pick you up. I love you! I just don't want anything thing to happen to you baby!" says Michelle. Aaron heeding to Michelle's advice reluctantly calls 911 for assistance. "911 may I help you?" says the 911dispatcher. Aaron hyperventilating shouts in the phone. I need an officer to 35408 Cherry Blossom Lane. I received a call about that my sister was in a serious accident but I can't go because my wife thinks that this is a setup to kill me, "says Aaron frantically. My name is Aaron Williams and I really need an officer over here now!" Aaron replies urgently. The dispatcher hearing the urgency of the call dispatches an officer to the Williams' residence. The dispatcher calmly speaks to Aaron. "I am sending an officer to your residence. Stay on the phone with me until they arrive" she says.

Moments later the officer arrives at the Williams' home responding to the call of someone calling about Aaron's sister being injured. Inviting the officer in the house Michelle explains the details of the call to 911. The officer aware of the planned murder plot probes Michelle for more information. "Did you recognize the voice of the caller?" the officer asks. Michelle looking the officer in the eye responds back nervously. "No sir, I never heard the voice before. He had a deep voice and seems to have been trying to muzzle it with his hand," says Michelle. The officer gets on his radio to explain the situation with his Commander on duty. After a brief conversation the commander and officer devised a plan to thwart a possible murder attempt to harm Aaron. Calling Aaron and Michelle together the officer explains the plan that the commander wants to execute. The officer looks at Aaron and puts his hand on his shoulder. "Mr. Williams we would like for you to drive your car to the hospital's emergency room parking lot. In the meantime we will have two unmarked police cars follow you in surveillance for anybody in the vicinity. At the hospital the commander will have officers positioned in detail to protect you if this is a plan to get you to the hospital to attempt harm you. What makes this seems like a murder plot is that our 911 management system hasn't received a call about an accident involving a female in the last twelve hours. In addition our paramedics haven't reported transporting anyone involved in an accident over the last two hours. What I want you to do is go to your car and follow the lead unmarked car to the hospital. I will be in direct communication with you on your cell phone." he says. Mrs. Williams if you can stay here while we carry this plan out we would appreciate it," says the officer. Upset that she can't be with her husband Michelle replies. "Officer I want to be with my husband.

He needs me to be with him," she pleads. Understanding that she wants to be with her husband the officer responds again. It's best that you don't come along," says the officer understanding her plight.

As Aaron heads down the freeway with several unmarked police cars escorting him he nears the hospital exit. Taking the exit to the light Aaron makes a left turn. Aaron realizing that the hospital emergency parking lot is only two blocks starts to get very nervous. Knowing that he has protection around him Aaron slowly turns into the emergency parking entrance where a bright red sign greets him. As he began to park his vehicle a burgundy Honda Civic pulls up next to him. Immediately the plain-clothes officers come from all directions converge on the vehicle with their guns drawn pointed at Joe, the hit man hired by Kim to murder Aaron. "Get your damn hands on the steering wheel and don't move!" shouts an officer at Joe. In compliance Joe sits there in a moment of paralysis fearing that he will be shot from one of the six weapons pointed at his head. Escorting Aaron away from the scene to avoid any more traumas the officers' snatches open the driver's side door. Pulling Joe out of the vehicle onto the ground, the officers puts him on the ground handcuffing him. The shift commander gets a visual identification of him and instructs his officers to place him in the squad car and transport him to the interrogation room at headquarters. The commander then goes over to Aaron who is deeply emotional and exasperated and places his hand on his shoulder. "Mr. Williams thanks for your cooperation. I know it wasn't easy but I think we solved this situation that I know had you and your family on edge. You can leave as soon as we get a little more information from you," says the officer. I know is worried and want you to get back home," he says with a smile. Leaving the scene Aaron immediately calls his wife who is crying on the phone. "Baby, baby I'm okay," says Aaron his voice cracking as he slows down driving fearful that he is going to have an accident. "I almost got killed, "Aaron tries to explain the details but his emotions were interfering with him being able to finish his sentences. Michelle understanding that her husband has been through a traumatizing ordeal pleads with him to just drive safely home. "Aaron please drive home safely, we will talk about it when you get here. Okay?" she says slowing her words down so Aaron who is frantic could understand her clearly. After ending her call with Aaron, Michelle gets back on the phone calling Pastor Wright for assistance knowing that her husband will be an emotionally wreck when he arrives home. After three rings Pastor Wright answers the phone. Hello, this is Pastor Wright may I help you?" he asks in his most prophetic voice. Michelle very anxious over Aaron's situation replies. "Pastor Wright this is Michelle Williams. I need your help immediately," she says urgently. Realizing that Michelle has an emergency Pastor Wright attempts to slow her down so he can understand her request. "Michelle slow down and tell me what's going on?" he says encouragingly. Michelle at the request of the Pastor attempts to explain her plea again. "Pastor Wright Aaron just went through a major ordeal at the hospital where a person was sitting in a car outside of his home planning kill him. He was with the police who stopped him from getting killed. Aaron is on his way home and he is an emotional wreck when I talked to him on his phone. He was having a difficult time driving so I got off the phone before he had an accident. Could you please come over to the house before he gets here, please!" she pleads. Pastor Wright understanding her request and urgency responds. "Michelle I'm on my way," he says hanging up the phone.

CHAPTER 12

One week after the Federal Drug Enforcement Administration served a search warrant on the Remington Corporation the grand jury of the U.S. Federal Court indicted Robert Remington Sr. on one count of each which includes illegal drug trafficking, illegal wiretapping, bank fraud and tax evasion. If convicted of all charges Mr. Remington Sr. could face up to 120 years in prison. The DEA with the cooperation of state, county and local law enforcement announced that it is continuing its investigation of others who may be involved in illegal activities related to the drug trafficking. Hearing that he had been indicted on the charges Mr. Remington accompanied by his attorneys turned himself into authorities the next day. After hearing the charges before the defendant the Judge sets Mr. Remington's bond at million dollar cash. The Judge also ordered the defendant's to appear for a preliminary hearing in two weeks.

Appearing in U.S. Federal Court for his preliminary hearing before Judge Alvin Spalding, Robert Remington Sr. stands very still. Flanked by his attorneys in the cavernous looking courtroom Judge Spalding looks over at the Federal Prosecutor Michael Sweeney as he motions to court personnel that he was ready to start the hearing. As the Judge prepares to read off the charges the courtroom including Robert's family and staff along with the media gets very quiet.

This is cases number 18-1884, 18-1885, 19-1886, 18-1887, the United States vs. Robert Remington Sr. May I hear accounts of the indictments says the Judge looking over at the Prosecutor. Stepping up to the microphone wearing a navy blue suit Prosecutor Michael Sweeney flips through volumes of neatly stacked papers on the podium. "Your honor, before you are cases 18-1884, 1985, 1986. 1987 brought against Mr. Remington that includes drug trafficking, illegal wiretapping, bank fraud and income tax evasion. These charges were under a sealed indictment while the Drug Enforcement Administration's agents intensified their efforts of surveillance of Robert Remington Sr. and his company known as the Remington Corporation that was being used to hide and launder illegal drug money. This investigation started weeks ago but couldn't be finalized until April 2, 2018 based on knowledge of three individuals who came to the DEA office with a complaint of drug activity at the Remington Corporation. The Drug Enforcement Administration after receiving this complaint and knowing that if they didn't act quickly on this complaint that any delay could potential smear this investigation acted quickly. Their agency with the assistance of the Miami police along with the Federal Prosecutor's office asked the courts to unseal the above mentioned indictments and request that the Judge sign a search warrant to seize computer software and telecommunication equipment out of the Remington Corporation's offices. After getting the required signatures a search was executed without incident on April 4, 2018 at 9:00 a.m. at the Remington Corporation. During the search Robert Remington Sr. was arrested and charged. That's all we have right now your honor," says Federal prosecutor Sweeney before as he goes back to his table to take a seat. Hearing the affidavit in its entirety Judge Whitman turns his attention to the defendant and counsel. "Counsel, how does your client plead to the charges?" Attorney Michael Strickland, legal counsel for Robert Remington Sr. speaks without hesitation. "Your honor, my client is pleading not guilty of all charges," he says looking over at Mr. Remington. As Judge Spalding makes several notes on a pad in front of him and types in information on his laptop computer that sits to the right of him he looks up and stares at the defense attorney. "I accept the defendant's not guilty pleas on all the before mentioned charges. Looking at his computer deciding a date for a scheduled trial date Judge Spalding looks up at the Prosecutor and Defense Attorney. How is June 11th for both of you?" he asks the Prosecutor and the Defense Attorney. The Prosecutor after looking at his schedule responds immediately. "Your honor I'm available," Immediately after defense attorney Strickland responds with a question for the Judge before committing a trial date. "Your honor, how long do you expect this trial to last?" asks staring at his calendar again. Judge Spalding looks at counsel with pen in hand. "I would give it at least three weeks counsel," he says openly. Attorney smiles and nods affirmatively at the Judge. "That date works for me your honor." Confirming the trial date in his computer the Judge looks up at the Prosecutor. "Is there anything regarding bond from prosecution," he asks. The Prosecutor stands up from his table. "Your honor, in regards to bond we are requesting a very high bond for the defendant. Our request is based on the level of the drug trade that was involved and the seriousness of this drug activity. Even though Mr. Remington has been a successful businessman in this community we deem him as a flight risk if given a low or attainable bond," says Prosecutor Sweeney. Making notes Judge Spalding turns his attention to defense counsel. Counsel do you have anything regarding bond? Attorney Strickland stands up from behind the defense table next to Mr. Remington. "Your honor, defense is asking for a reasonable bond for my client on the allegations of which he has pleaded not guilty. Mr. Remington is a lifelong resident of Miami and a successful businessman and pillar in our community. My client has a corporation that is very successful. Just this year Mr. Remington received an award from the Fortune 500 Commission for his business placing in the top 500 for profitable businesses in the nation. Mr. Remington is not a flight risk to leave the country. He has a loving family and a wife who is battling breast cancer that he needs to be with. In lieu of this we're asking for a reasonable bond," says the attorney. After a few moments of thought and self-deliberations Judge Whitman comes with his decision. "I have deemed this case a very serious one based on the type of allegations that has been presented before the court. Reviewing the records and all that was shared by both counsels Judge Whitman makes his decision. "I will continue bond at one million dollars. The defendant is also ordered to surrender his passport. The time allowed will give him time to get his business affairs in order and be with his wife until the trial starts. Mr. Remington you are not to have any dealings with anyone who is doing illegal practices including drug activity. Last but not least you are to report to my courtroom with your attorney on June 14, 2018 at 9:00 A.M. in Room 222. If there is no other judicial action I need to address regarding this case this hearing is adjourned," says the Judge as he picks up his legal file and head back to his chambers.

CHAPTER 13

Preparing to be discharged from his twenty one day stay at the rehab facility, Rob Jr. is surprised to see his mom and sister visiting him. Deena, carrying a bouquet of flowers, balloons and a card approaches Rob and gives him a hug as well as his mom. Rob looking well after weeks of treatment smiles. "How did you know I was getting out," he asks curiously. Deena looks at him sarcastically and smiles. Like there is no way to check on you crazy," she says. I was checking up on you every week even though I wasn't making visits. Remember I am your sister and she is your mother right?" she says laughing. Walking up and giving her brother another hug Deena's gets emotional. Rob, seeing his sister crying starts getting emotional which is very seldom by his family. "Sister I never thought you cared this much for me. Especially since I became an alcoholic," he says. Deena takes Rob hands and places them in hers and smiles. Rob, regardless of what you have been going through I am your sister and I love you. You have disappointed me at times but I never lost my love for you. Mom and I got some good news for you and some not so good news for you today," she says openly. "Which one would you want to hear first?" she asks. Rob nervous to both options looks at her sarcastically.

"Let's hear the good news. I haven't heard good news in so long that it may bring me closer to God," he says laughing. And you know how long it has been since I've believed in God. Deena looks at shaking her head before asking her to tell him the news. "Mom why don't you tell Rob the good news first," she says. Sarah looks at her son with a glowing smile. "First I want to share the great news that I am cancer free! I had a checkup this week and my Oncologist said I am free of breast cancer," says Sarah smiling while tearing up. The other good news is that you no longer will you have to stay at that halfway house. Deena and I have leased you a furnished the apartment with rent paid for six months until you find a job. We also started you a bank account," she says. Rob shocked at what his sister and mom has done looks at both in sincere appreciation. "You didn't have to do this for me. Now what's the bad news? I know, they called you back and told you that they couldn't rent to a recovering alcoholic, huh?" he says in laughter. Deena intervenes immediately. No Rob, they can't discriminate against you because you're in recovery. However, we have some not so good news regarding dad," she says staring him in the eye. Rob, thinking that his dad is gravely ill looks numb at Deena waiting for her to share the bad news. Deena, struggling emotionally to tell him what's going on begins to cry. "Well Rob, dad was indicted on some criminal activity that he was alleged to be involved in two weeks ago. He was charged with drug trafficking, money laundering and attempted murder for hire," she says. Looking at his mom holding her head down seemingly depressed he stands stoic to what he just heard. Rob gathers himself and shares with his sister. "Well, if there is a God I hope that he will help mom because dad is getting what he deserves," he says without hesitation. Deena staring at Rob angrily responds regarding the comments he made in front of mom raises her voice. "Rob, how can say such damaging words while mom is here? That's her husband that you're making those ridiculous and slanderous comments toward. Look at your mom crying! You should be ashamed of yourself! You owe her an apology right now!" she says holding back her tears. Rob shakes his head sadly. "I wish I could feel a certain way but I can't. The way dad treated me when I came over for dinner was the last straw," he says. Deena looks at Rob staring at him. Have you ever heard of the word forgiveness? Even though you don't believe in God the bible says forgive those who trespass against you and show them mercy. I know dad hasn't been perfect nor has you Rob. Right now dad needs you more than ever. He swears that the charges brought against him are not true. I have no reason don't to believe him. We can say what we want but dad is not a liar. After you leave this center why don't you practice the act of forgiveness? Obviously somebody forgave you over the years for all the sinful things you have to others," she says. Handing the keys and lease papers to the apartment, and banking account papers to Rob she pleads with him. "I know you and dad's relationship is bad but hopefully in the near future I can sit down with both of you and find peace," she says as she and her mom leaves the center.

CHAPTER 14

Walking into the Remington Corporation doors after a two-week hiatus was a weird feeling for Aaron. Not sure what type of reception he would get, Aaron walks into the office. Arriving at the Receptionist desk he smiles at Camille. "Well hello Camille," he says hoping to get the radiant smile he normally receives every morning. Camille, forcing a smile greets Aaron before returning to her typing. "Hello Aaron," she says casually. Feeling something was wrong he walks away heading to his office. Moments before he arrives to his office door Camille interrupts him. "Aaron, Oh I forgot to mention to you that there has been some changes here at the office. Mr. Remington last week changed your office. Your office is now next to the supply room. He had a moving company come in and make the changes," she says knowing that Aaron would be very upset. Aaron seemingly unmoved emotionally by the change smiles at Camille before going to his new office. Walking in his office he notices his furniture and personal items cluttered in the office that is half the size of the office he previously occupied. Pulling out his chair from the desk he squeezes his body forcefully into the seat. Looking at his desk phone he notices that all of his messages that he had received were deleted. Finding it difficult to work under these conditions he decides that he will leave for the day until he can mentally assess if he should come back to work at the Remington Corporation. Aaron gets up from his chair and grabs his brief case and leaves out of his office door closing it behind him. Walking out to the reception area he speaks to Camille briefly. "I'm leaving for the day. I need time to decide my future with this company," he says obviously upset of his work environment. Camille, feeling bad for Aaron understands how difficult it is for him to be moved apologizes. "Aaron I'm sorry." she says getting out of her chair and around her desk to give him a hug. "I knew last week that something wasn't right. Detectives were here several weeks ago with search warrants going through you and Mr. Remington's office. I had no idea what was going on," she said obviously depressed about what had happened. "I do Camille but all I can tell you to do is pray for everyone here," says Aaron before walking out of the office. Walking to the elevators Aaron is met by Mr. Remington coming off the elevator going to his office. Confronting Aaron angrily Mr. Remington who walks up to him and physically pushes up against him. "I can't believe you done this to me! I can't believe you would turn on me for all that I have done for you," he says angrily. Aaron, making every attempt to explain that he didn't accuse him of anything stares at his boss. "What are you talking about Mr. Remington?" he asks. "You know what I'm talking about you son of as bitch! Why did you call the feds on me? I want you to get everything that belongs to you out of your damn office and leave! Kim told me not to hire you in because you would try to take over my business and I didn't listen to her. You're the scum of the earth," he says walking away extremely upset. Aaron visually upset immediately gets on the elevator leaving in a confused state of mind. Getting into his car Aaron calls his wife on his cell phone. Hearing her husband's tone of voice Michelle could tell something was wrong. "What's wrong baby," she asks very concerned. "Michelle, I got some bad news. When I was leaving the office on the way to the elevator I was stopped by Mr. Remington who went into a verbal rage accusing me of trying to take over his corporation and calling the feds on him. He started screaming at me calling me all kinds of names and even told me to get everything out of my office. He fired me," said Aaron crying on the phone. Michelle seriously concerned about her husband's mental condition speaks to him in a calm manner. "Baby, where are you right now, she asks. replies. "I can't believe he would do something like this to you," obviously upset. Trying to keep her husband under emotional control she reassures him. "Baby don't worry, we will be okay. We've come too far to fail. Just come on home and we will come with a plan," she says confidently. As Aaron leaves the office tower and gets to his car he notices a piece of paper wedged between his windshield and wiper. Taking the paper off the glass Aaron gets in his car before reading the message. Shocked at what he is reading he immediately speeds out of the driveway. Driving somewhat erratically on the freeway Aaron takes the Paragon Avenue exit one mile away from his house. Turning into his driveway he immediately goes in his house making sure the door was locked before calling his wife. "I'm home baby," he says nervously. Upon hearing her husband's voice she goes and gives him a hug. "I'm so glad to see you baby.

Are you okay?" she asks staring him in the eye. Giving his wife an emotional hug he shares with her the threatening note he found on his windshield. "Michelle when I got to my car there was a note on my windshield saying that I needed to watch my back or I will be dead," he says somberly. Startled at his comments she immediately goes and gets the cordless phone receiver off the table and call the police. After several rings the police dispatcher answers. "Hello Miami Police." Michelle nervously responds. "Hello this is Michelle Williams at 35408 Cherry Blossom Lane. I need an officer to come to my residence right away," she says urgently. Curious to what the problem is the dispatcher probes for more answers. "What seems to be the problem?" she asks. "My husband Aaron Williams received a threatening note on his windshield as he was leaving work and we would like to have it investigated. Understanding, but still not clear of its severity the dispatcher replies. "I will send an officer over to your house," she said before hanging up. Taking her husband's hand and leading him to the family room Michelle sits next to him on the sofa. "Baby, I don't know why all these things are happening to us but through the grace of God we will get through it and have peace," she says squeezing his hand and giving him a kiss. Moments later there is a knock on the door. Expecting the police but wanting to make sure Michelle hollers out. "Who is it?" "Miami Police," says the officer. Walking quickly to the door Michelle opens it and greets the officers. "Hello officers come on in, "says Michelle nervously. She escorts the officer into the house into the family room. As Michelle and the officer arrive in the family room Aaron appears to be in a state of shock from the recent episodes of threats.

"Officer my husband Aaron has been through a lot over the last three weeks. Today he went to work and his boss threatened him demanding he get his personal items out of his office and leave," Michelle says raising her voice in a high pitch tone. Taking notes on a pad he took out of his shirt pocket the officer asks curiously. "So what I'm hearing is an argument ensued between your husband and his boss and he fired him," he asks. "No officer this is a situation where my husband found out that his boss may be involved with drug trafficking," she says. Looking at Aaron the officer directs his comments toward him. "So is this an incident that stems from the Remington indictments that came down several weeks ago?" the officer questions Aaron. Aaron stares at the officer his eyes glossy from being emotional. "Yes sir," he says. The officer places his pad in his pockets and walks around with Aaron then immediately stops and questions Aaron. "Do you still have the note on you?" Aaron reaches in his gray suit coat pocket, pulls out the note and hands it to the officer. Reading over the note the officer places it in a small folder. I'm going to take this paper to the crime lab to be finger printed," he says looking at both Aaron and Michelle. Contact us if anything else comes up," the officer says as he began to leave the home.

Preparing to be discharged from a forty-two day alcohol rehab inpatient admission, Rob Jr. is greeted by his mom and sister with a bouquet of flowers, balloons and a congratulation card. Shocked at his sister and mom's presence Rob smiles while looking vibrant and healthy from his impatient stay. "What are you guys doing here?" he asks forcing a smile. Deena looks at Rob sarcastically and smiles looking at her mom. "Well, I am your sister and she is your mom right?" she says laughing. Walking up and giving her brother a hug Deena steps back so Sarah can embrace her son as he becomes emotional. As tears began to stream down his face Rob he gets choked up attempting to express his feelings. "Deena I never thought you cared about me so much, especially since I became an alcoholic," says Rob. Deena takes Rob hands and places them in hers and smiles. Rob, regardless of what you were going through, I'm still your sister and I will always love you. I may have been disappointed but I never lost my love for you. Mom and I got some good news for you and some not so good news for you today," she says openly. "Which one would you want to hear first?" she asks. Rob nervous to both options looks at Deena eyes wide open. "Let's hear the good news. I haven't heard good news in so long that it may bring me closer to God. And you know how long it has been since I've believed in God. Deena looks at her mom smiling struggling to tell Rob the news. "Mom why don't you tell Rob the good news," she says delightfully. Sarah looks at Rob with a glowing smile. "Rob, Deena and I have found you an apartment on the west side of town that is so beautiful. We have paid your rent for a whole year. No longer will you have to stay at that halfway house. We also have furnished it with the most beautiful furniture and started you a bank account until you can find employment," she says as she gives her son another hug. Rob shocked at what his sister and mom has done looks at both in sincere appreciation. You didn't have to do this for me. Now what's the bad news? I know, they called you back and told you that they can't rent to a recovering alcoholic, huh?" he says in laughter.

Deena intervenes immediately. No Rob, they are not going to discriminate against you because you're in recovery. However, we have some bad news regarding dad," Deena said staring Rob in the eye. Rob thinking that his dad is gravely ill looks numb at Deena waiting for her to share the bad news. Deena struggling emotionally to tell Rob what's going on begins to cry. "Well Rob, dad was indicted on some criminal activity that he was alleged to be involved in three weeks ago. He was charged with drug trafficking and pandering a prostitution ring and attempted murder," she says. Looking at his mom holding her head down in shame Rob stands stoic to what he just heard. "If there is a God I hope that he will help mom Deena because dad is getting what he deserves," says Rob with a smile on his face. Deena staring at Rob extremely angry at his comment he made about his dad raises her voice at him. "Rob, how can say such damaging words while mom is here. That's her husband that you are making those ridiculous and slanderous comments toward. Look at your mom, look at her crying. You should be ashamed of your damn self. You owe her an apology right now," she says holding back her tears. Rob shakes his head sadly. 'No disrespect to mom but the bastard is getting what he deserves. The way he treated me and lied about what he was going to do for me. Mom should have left him a long time ago. Yeah I know, I know you did it for us so we wouldn't grow up without a daddy around like our friends in the neighborhood. Deena I can't believe you are in denial. You know we would have been better off if he wasn't around. We wouldn't have the emotional and physical scars that we are living with now. I hope he rots in jail," Rob says angrily. Protecting her mom's already fragile mental and emotional state while she is in remission with her breast cancer Deena gives Rob a death stare. Quickly ushering her mom out of the facility, Deena throws the apartment keys at Rob in anger. I hope before you die you learn the word forgiveness Rob," she says leaving slamming the door loudly.

CHAPTER 15

Arriving home from an exhausting and frightening experience Aaron walks in the door looking for his wife. "Michelle I'm home," he shouts out. Michelle hearing his voice from a distance walks rapidly to the living room. Seeing him exasperated and seemingly defeated from his ordeal she goes over and gives him a big hug and kiss. 'Baby I was so afraid that you wouldn't make it home. I even called Pastor Wright who said he will be over in a few hours," she says still embracing him again. Aaron is able to force a smile through it all walks over to the family room and takes a seat and a deep sigh of relief.

Moments later the doorbell rings causing Michelle to leave the family room to see who it may be. "Who is it?" she asks politely. "It's Pastor Wright," he replies. Quickly opening the door she greets the pastor with a warm embrace. "Thank you Pastor for coming over on such short notice. Aaron is in the family room a little shaken up from his ordeal. Come on in," she says escorting him into the living room. Walking in the room the Pastor makes eye contact with Aaron then walks over to greet him. Aaron stands up from the sofa as Pastor Wright embraces Aaron while whispering in his ear. "God bless you Aaron," he says they sit down. Feeling a sense of calmness in the air Michelle opens up the discussion by thanking the Pastor for coming by. "Pastor as you know, Aaron and I have been going through some extremely difficult times the past several weeks. You have been so supportive with your spiritual wisdom and prayers. Just when we thought things would get better we received a call today from an individual who said that he was a friend of Aaron's. He wouldn't identify himself by name but said that Aaron's sister was in a serious car accident and that he needed to come to University Hospital Emergency immediately. Unsure who the caller was I told them he wasn't here and tried to take a message. He wouldn't leave one but he had a husky voice that seemed to be muzzled by his hand. Aaron tried to call his sister to no avail which gave him the reason to believe that what he was saying was true. Because of the uncertainty regarding the call, I had him call the police. From here Aaron can tell you what happened after that," she says looking over at Aaron. Aaron nervously carries on the conversation by telling Pastor the ending details of his near encounter with death. "Well Pastor, the dispatcher informed me that one of their officers was on our street and she would send him over. Through the advice of the police commander they encouraged me to drive to the hospital emergency room parking lot with two unmarked police cars in front and back of me. Once we arrived to the emergency room parking lot I saw a Caucasian man in a faded burgundy Honda pulled up next to me. At that point the police swarmed his vehicle with guns out placing him under arrest," he says as he recounts the situation. The Pastor hearing the dramatic accounts of what he went through encourages Aaron and Michelle to come closer to him. Taking their hands hand he asked them to join him in prayer. After a brief prayer the pastor advises them to stay close to each other and pray daily. Looking at his watch Pastor Wright realizes that he is almost running late for his next appointment gives Aaron and Michelle an embrace before leaving.

Later in the afternoon after being processed at the detention center Joe is brought in brightly lit interrogation room at the justice center. Handcuffed and in his green inmate jumpsuit Joe squirms in his seat trying to adjust the handcuffs that were placed on his wrist tightly. Walking up to Joe demanding answers Detective Lawson stares at him. Tell me Mr. Fields who you operating with?" says the detective pacing the floor. Joe looks up at the detective angrily. "I said nobody!" Walking up close to Joe giving him little breathing room he calmly asks his question again. I am going to ask you one more time. Who you operating with!' he says literally screaming in Joe's face. Twisting in his chair uncomfortable Joe responds again. "I said nobody!" Literally screaming to his lungs again the detective slams a chair on the floor making an echo in the room. "I've been on the force for over thirty years and I know when I'm being lied too! If you want to take the fall by yourself, that's fine. It will be your ass in the slammer!" says the detective pacing around thinking of another investigated tactic to use on Joe. "Mr. Fields, are you're aware that you can possibly face twenty years if you are convicted on these charges. However being the caring detective I'm willing to cut you a deal. If you tell me who else was involved in this murder plot I can help you get less time on some of these charges, maybe probation" he says. Joe, still aching in discomfort from the handcuffs laughs at the detective. "You must think I'm a fool. You all say that then have me going up the river," he says laughing.

Moments later the detective uses a tactic that has worked in the past and fakes like he is receiving a call on his cell phone. "This is Detective Lawson. Acting as he is listening to information being shared the detective and hangs up his cell phone. Looking at Joe smiling as if he has received new information the detective speaks. "Mr. Fields I hate to tell you this but all bets are off," he says directly. I now know who was involved. Joe listening intently to the detective nervously raises his head up and stares at the detective. "What are you talking about?" he asks curious to the detective's motives. The detective walks away from Joe then turns around. "We already know who was involved in this murder plot with you. Now do you want to voluntarily tell me who else is involved so I can make it easy on you," says the detective. Feeling that the detective is playing games Joe laughs again. "Man you think I'm going to fall for the old phone call trick," he says. The detective looks at Joe curiously. "Mr. Fields do you know a person by the name of Ralph? That's right Ralph Wilson, your middle man who arranged this murder for hire plot for you," he says adamantly. Realizing that the detective knows more than he thought Joe starts to think more about the stance he is taking. "Okay, what's the deal if I talk?" says Joe curiously. The detective knowing that he has Joe where he wants him responds. "What do you want to tell me that I already don't know?" says Detective Lawson. Conceding, Joe spills the beans on his accomplices. "I was called by a friend name Ralph Wilson who told me that he needed me to take out a person who was causing trouble," says Joe. Getting more into his interrogation the detective digs deeper into his questions. Tell me more about this Ralph Wilson guy and who was his contact," asks Lawson. Joe takes a pause then replies. "He was doing a job for a woman name Kim at the Remington Company. They wanted me to take out this black guy who works there. I was told that he knew too much so they were going to paid me five thousand dollars after I did the job," he said hoping that his snitching will get him a break on his sentence. "So are you are willing to testify to this in court," the detective asks staring at Joe. Hearing Joe's taped confession Detective Lawson radios the police dispatcher to send several officers to come to the interrogation room to take Joe back to the county jail.

Completing their investigation the Regional Police Department compiles information to submit to the Prosecutor to present to the grand jury. Four days later the grand jury handed down criminal indictments on Ralph Wilson, Kim Downing and Joe Fields. As days linger on Aaron unsure of his ability to go back to work contacts the Police Department to see if it is safe to return to work. Speaking with the Police Chief, he wants to get a status report on their investigation on the murder plot since he was almost a victim. Hoping he can return to work, he speaks to the Chief. 'Hello Chief my name is Aaron Williams. I was the person that was getting ready to be killed at the hospital by a person who was planning on murdering me. Your officers did a great job apprehending the person. Since then I have been apprehensive about going to work because of my safety. I want to know if you think if it is okay to return to work." he asks. The Chief, listening to

Aaron's question responds honestly. "Mr. Williams based on my reports from my shift commander it appears we have arrested the individual responsible for the crime. We think you are okay to return to work," he says. After the Prosecutor presented evidence based on statements to the grand jury by the Prosecutor indictments were handed down charging Ralph Lowell for racketeering. Also indicted was David Richburg charged with one count of illegal wiretapping. After several weeks of intense searching both suspects were apprehended and process at the county jail. At their hearing both Ralph and David pleaded not guilty to their charges and given bonds and a trial date.

CHAPTER 16

Walking in the courtroom dressed in a blue pinstripe suit flanked by his two prominent attorneys Michael Strickland and Joseph Caudill, Mr. Remington takes a seat at the defense table smiling at his family sitting nearby. Looking around the cavernous high ceiling, the courtroom gives an intimidating presence to all that are present. As courtroom staff hurries to get their documents in place before court is officially in session Remington appears jittery. The federal bailiff gets the attention of everyone in the courtroom. "Court is in session. The Honorable Judge Alvin Spalding of the United States Federal Court presiding." As Judge Spalding walks into the courtroom from his chambers to his bench he is greeted by court personnel. Taking a seat the Judge instructs those in his courtroom. "Welcome," he says in a gravely strong voice while shuffling through his papers inserted in his legal file folder. Looking up at the Prosecutor and defense attorneys then to the federal marshals assigned to the court trial. "Please bring the jurors into the courtroom." Moments later twelve jurors are escorted to the jury box where they all are seated. Judge Spalding looks at the jurors smiling. "Welcome to U.S. Federal Court. I would like to proceed with this case. I have given the jurors for this trial their instructions and judicial protocols related to this case. Looking over at the administrator of Court Services and receiving positive acknowledgment that all has been completed with court protocol Judge Spalding continues. "We are regarding case numbers 18-1884, 1885, 1886, 1887 the United States vs. Robert Remington Sr. Robert Remington Sr. has been formally charged and indicted on one count of drug trafficking, one count of complicity to attempted murder, one count of illegal wiretapping and one count of obstruction of justice. After peering over wire rimmed glasses at the both counsel's table making sure they are ready the Judge opens. "Let's start with opening statements from the prosecution," says Judge Spalding. As the Prosecutor Michael Flowers gets up from the table and positions himself between the Judge and the jurors he began his opening statements. "Good morning your honor and members of the jury, before you is a very complicated and somewhat unusual criminal case involving a high profile defendant by the name of Robert Remington Sr. who is charged with four federal indictments. One count each of attempted drug trafficking, one count of illegal wire-tapping, one count of complicity to attempt murder and one count of obstruction of justice. This trial is a direct result of a federal investigation that started seven months ago but was later stalled by the lack of true information that the government received from individuals connected to this case. However two months ago after receiving what the DEA and the Miami Police Department believed was credible information from a complaint involving illegal activity at the Remington Corporation the investigation restarted. The complaint involved voicemail conversations from the Remington Corporation through what was believed to have been sent through the corporation's President/CEO, Mr. Remington's telephone. The voice mail clearly involves illegal drug dealings at the corporation. It is believed that the corporation was used as a shield to hide drugs and money. The United States Drug Enforcement Agency requested and received a federal Judge's signed search warrant to execute a search of said property called the Remington Corporation. On April 4, 2018 agents from the United States Drug Enforcement Agency served a search warrant and physically search and removed two computers, notes and four cell phones and a box of documents from the offices of the Remington Corporation. Two days later on April 6, 2018 the Dade County Grand Jury handed down a four count indictment accusing the defendant Robert Remington Sr., President/CEO on charges of attempted drug trafficking, mail fraud, illegal wiretapping, and complicity to commit murder and obstruction of justice. On April 6, 2018 Robert Remington Sr. was arraigned in U. S. Federal Court on the above mentioned charges and pleaded not guilty to all charges and was released on a million dollar bond. In addition the Judge at the preliminary hearing ordered that the defendant give up his international passport and not leave the country without the permission of the United States District Court. The government will present evidence both material and testimony to prove without a reasonable doubt that the defendant Robert Remington Sr. is guilty of the charges he has been charged. That's all I have right now, your honor and members of the jury," says the Prosecutor. The courtroom remains silent as Prosecutor Flowers goes back to his seat. Judge Spalding makes notes on his personal computer before looking over at the defense table. "Counsel, you can start with your opening statements," says the Judge. Attorney Strickland, a prominent defense attorney from California hired by Remington to handle his case gets up from his chair and approaches the bench acknowledging the Judge and the jurors. "Good morning, your honor and members of the jury. In do respect what I heard the opening statements from the prosecution and listened intently to the allegations. I would like to start off by saying that the information you just heard from the plaintiff is exactly what it is, an allegation. The charges that were levied against my client Robert Remington Sr. are mere accusations in an attempt to discredit and destroy a business icon in this community. As we proceed through this trial I will be able to show you through testimony, cross examinations and time graphs that my client is not guilty of the charges being presented to you this morning. If you pay close attention to all aspects of our delivery in this trial we will show you that our client is being used in an organized drug operation to tarnish his image and destroy his corporation that he has built over the years. With that we have no other statements at this time," says Attorney Strickland before going back to his seat. Judge Spalding reviews his notes taken after listening to the defense opening statements. Raising his head looking in the direction of the prosecution Judge Spalding speaks clearly. "Counsel you can present any prosecution evidence and witnesses before the court," says Judge Spalding. Your honor and members of the jury I would like to direct your attention to the table to the far left says Prosecutor Flowers pointing in the direction of the evidence. On that table you will see physical evidence, which includes a computer and two telephones which was confiscated in the search warrant. Your honor we would like the evidence here to be known as Exhibit A and Exhibit B," says Flowers. Judge Spalding responds. Items involving the two computers that were confiscated from the Remington Corporation as part of a search warrant will be allowed as evidence and be known as Exhibit A. Items involving the two telephones that were confiscated from the Remington Corporation from a search warrant will be allowed as evidence and be known as Exhibit B. The Prosecutor smiles at the Judge then looks at the jurors. "Thank you your honor," he says. "The computers and phones that you see were sent to the national crime lab for examination. It was determined through the lab's expert forensic technicians that more information will be resented as they continue their findings. But what we do know is a wide spread and sophisticated drug trafficking operation that originated in Mexico and ended up being orchestrated at the business known as the Remington Corporation. Immediately Attorney Strickland gets out of his chair objecting to the Prosecutor's comments. "I object your honor to the Prosecutor's statements that my client's business is involved in a drug operation. He has no proof and his comments are baseless," says Strickland. After hearing the objection the Judge responds. "Objection sustained, strike the comments from prosecution of the Remington Corporation being a part of a drug operation," says the Judge. "Prosecution, please continue," says the Judge. Standing behind his table Prosecutor Flowers responds to the Judge's request. Your honor to support my earlier statements of the Remington Corporation's involvement in this operation I would like to bring our key witness Aaron Williams to the stand," say Flowers. Looking directly at the Prosecutor the Judge responds. "You may have your witness come to the witness stand," say Spalding. Aaron sitting near the back row gives his wife a long embrace and hug to Pastor Wright. Walking to the front of the courtroom wearing a tailored black three-piece suit, Aaron approaches by the court bailiff who is ready to give him instructions. "Do you swear to tell the truth, nothing but the truth so help me God?" Aaron responds back nervously. "I do," says Aaron. "You may be seated," says the Bailiff directing him to the seat in the witness stand inside the wooden rail cubicle. As Aaron is seated the Prosecutor Flowers began to speak to Aaron. "Mr. Williams for the record say your first and last name and spell it," he asks pleasantly. "My name is Aaron Williams A-A-R-O-N W-I-L-L-I-A-M-S," says Aaron. Pacing with his ink pen front of him Flowers stops in front of Aaron. "Mr. Williams, it is my understanding that you are employed with the Remington Corporation is that correct," asks Flowers. "Yes," responds Aaron. "And what is your position with the Remington Corporation," Flowers asks. "I am the Vice President of Business Operations," Aaron responds. "And it is my understanding that you work under the direct supervision of the Mr. Robert Remington Sr. is that correct?" asks Flowers. Aaron nods affirmatively. "Yes sir." Looking around the courtroom and then at Aaron Prosecutor Flowers directs another question to him. "Mr. Williams, do you see Mr. Remington Sr. in the courtroom?" Aaron again nods affirmatively at the Prosecutor. Yes sir." Staring at Aaron, Flowers questions him again. "Can you point him out and tell us what he is wearing?" he asks smiling. "Yes, he is the gentleman sitting at the brown table and wearing a blue pinstripe suit," Aaron says nervously attempting to avoid making contact with his boss. Judge Spalding speaks up immediately. "Let the record reflect that the witness Aaron Williams identified the defendant Robert Remington Sr. You may continue counsel." Prosecutor Flowers smiles at Aaron. "Thank you. Mr. Williams. On March 30, 2018 at 8:00 A.M. where were you" asked Flowers. Aaron sits up straight looking out at his wife. "I was in the reception area of the Remington Corporation going to my office," he says. Prosecutor Flowers stares at Aaron. "Mr. Williams did you have conversation with anyone when you arrived in the reception area at the Remington Corporation?" asks the Prosecutor. Aaron responds immediately. "Yes sir, I was greeted by our Receptionist and I asked her if I had received any calls," says Aaron. Prosecutor Flowers angles himself between Aaron and the jury. "What is the name of the receptionist" asks the Prosecutor seeking more information. "Her name is Camille" says Aaron nervously. Prosecutor Flowers walks closely towards Aaron. "And what was her response Mr. Williams?" he asks. "She said that she had sent four voice mail messages to my phone," says Aaron. Prosecutor Flowers looks at the jury before asking his next question. "Isn't it unusual that you would receive that many voice messages on your phone in a short period of time?" Aaron looks at the Prosecutor nervously not knowing where he was going with that question. "Yes sir," Aaron says quietly. Prosecutor Flowers smiles faintly then stares at Aaron deftly. "When you started listening to your voice mails from your phone and realized the content of the messages with words like "keys" and "stacking money" being delivered what was your first thoughts," asked the Prosecutor. "I was confused and I realized that the message was not for me," said Aaron. "And what did you after hearing the message," asks Flowers. "After hearing those words "keys" and "stacking money" and not knowing what they meant in reference to the message I decided to call my friend Lamont," he says. Flowers paces the floor then turns back to Aaron. "I assume that your friend Lamont knows that type of language what you heard in the message," says Flowers. "Yes sir. He said that keys meant kilogram which is the amount of drugs. And stacking money is hiding money usually made from selling drugs", says Aaron. The Prosecutor immediately responds. "Did your friend Lamont say anything else to you in reference to your conversation with him," he asks. "Yes, he told me that he think that somebody at my job was dealing drugs big time because and I needed to don't get caught up and get in trouble, especially if it is coming to your phone. You can be implicated," says Aaron. "So what did you do Mr. Williams," he asks. "I called my wife immediately and told her what was going on and went home for the day," he said. "So you did not report it to anyone at the company," asks Flowers. "No, I was scared to tell anyone there because of I didn't know who may be involved," says Aaron. "Not even Mr. Williams," he asks. "No sir, he says. Prosecutor Flowers walks away from Aaron then turns to the Judge and responds. "I have no further questions your honor," says Flowers returning back to his table. Taking a moment to write information down Judge Spalding looks up at the defense table. "Any cross examination from defense counsel," asks the Judge. Lead Attorney Strickland stands up and approaches the witness stand. "Mr. Williams, not to be repetitive but I heard you say that you didn't tell anyone at the Remington Corporation about the messages," says Strickland. "Yes sir, says Aaron. "Not even Mr. Remington, the one that hired you and the one who recently acknowledge you for your excellence job performance giving you a large bonus," said the attorney. "I object your honor to the State asking questions that are irrelevant and have nothing to do with the integrity of this case. Judge Spaulding looks over his wire rim glasses staring at Attorney Strickland. "Objection sustained, you may continue Counsel says the Judge wiping his eye brows. Strickland smiles at the Prosecutor before returning to his seat next to his client. Disappointed that the Judge did not allow his question as part of court record continues his interrogation. "Mr. Williams why didn't you tell your boss about what you heard on your voice messages unless you thought Mr. Remington was involved in this illegal activity," asks the attorney. Looking at the Judge Attorney Strickland responds." That's all I have your honor," says Strickland going back to his seat at the defense table. Allowing both counsels to get the paper work in order Judge Spalding looks out in the courtroom and delivers a message. "We will take a twenty minute recess, than we will come back and resume questioning of other witnesses.

CHAPTER 17

After a brief recess Judge Spalding comes back into the courtroom and takes a seat waiting for everyone to get seated. "Let's continue with the questioning of witnesses. Directing his attention toward the defense table the Judge continues the court hearing. Counsel, you can go ahead with your calling of witnesses," says Spalding. Strickland rise up slowly then look at the Judge before coming around from the table. "I would like to call Detective Lawson to the stand," says the attorney. Walking over to the jury members getting their attention Attorney Strickland looks back at the detective. Detective Lawson, where were you on June 8, 2018 at approximately 2:00 p.m.," asks Strickland. I was at University Hospital part of an undercover surveillance operation," he says. "Can you tell the court what type of situation it was that you were involved," asks Strickland. "Yes, we got a tip that a person was planning a murder. The plan was to call the individual to tell them that his sister was in a bad car accident and that he needed to come to the emergency room," he said. "Do you see the person who was targeted to be murdered in the courtroom detective," he asks. "Yes, he is the black man sitting in the rear of the courtroom in the black suit, says the detective. "For the record the person the detective is referring to is Aaron Williams. Detective Lawson, during this surveillance was a suspected apprehended," asks Strickland. "Yes sir," says Lawson. "What was the suspect charged with detective," asks the attorney. "He was charges with complicity to attempt murder," say Detective Lawson. Attorney Strickland paces the floor then turns his attention back to the detective. Hmm, complicity to murder meaning that someone else was involved right," asks Strickland. Yes sir," he responds. "Is the other person in this alleged murder plot in anyway my client Robert Remington Sr.," asks Attorney Strickland. "No sir," says the detective. Smiling as he walks toward the Judge. "That's all I have your honor," says the attorney as he goes and takes a seat whispering in Mr. Remington's ear. A buzz goes over the courtroom after hearing the reply from the detective that did not involve Remington in the suspected murder for hire. It was a noise that the Judge had to caution those in the courtroom. The Judge looks over at the Prosecutor curiously. Counsel is you planning to cross examine the witness," he asks. "No your honor," says Prosecutor Flowers looking dejected from the response from the detective. Defense counsel, do you have any more witnesses to present to the court," asks Judge Spalding. "Attorney Strickland gets up from his seat with a smile feeling that he has the case won responds to the Judge's request. Your honor the defense would like to bring to the stand Joe Fields. Unfortunately our witness is in detention. I would like to ask if the court will have a brief recess to allow the deputies to bring Mr. Fields to your courtroom," asks Strickland. Judge Strickland looks at his clock sitting on his table and responds. "We will have a ten minute recess then proceed. I ask that all involved in this case do not leave the area," he says.

After a brief recess Judge Spalding walks back into the courtroom and calls court back in session. As the attorneys prepare for their court proceedings Judge Spalding responds. "Will defense counsel call their next witness. "Your honor, defense will like to call Joe Fields to the witness stand," says Attorney Spalding. The Judge looks at the courtroom security." Deputy you may bring Joe Fields into the courtroom and escort him to the witness stand," says the Judge. The deputy goes to a nearby room adjacent to the courtroom to bring Joe into the courtroom. Leading him near the witness stand Joe is met by the court Bailiff who asks him to raise his right hand. "You swear to tell the truth, nothing but the truth so help me God," says the Bailiff. Joe starts at the Bailiff and responds. "I do," says Joe. As Joe takes a seat Attorney Strickland gets up from his defense table and walks over to the witness stand. "Mr. Fields, it is reported that you were hired in a plan to commit a murder against an employee of the Remington Corporation is that correct," ask the Attorney Strickland. Yes sir," replies Joe. Mr. Fields is the person that you were hired to murder in the courtroom today, asks the attorney. "Yes, it's the black man in the black suit in the back of the courtroom," he says pointing directly at Aaron. Attorney Strickland walks facing the jurors then turns his attention back to Joe. "Can you tell the court whom you negotiated this murder for hire to kill Mr. Williams," he asks while staring at the Judge. "I was contacted by a friend Ralph Wilson. He told me a lady name Kim wanted a hit out on a person she worked with," says Joe. Then what happened? Did you meet her," asks Strickland.

"Did you meet Kim, ask Strickland. "Yes, we met at a restaurant downtown," he said. "Then what happened," he asks. We discussed plans for me to murder Aaron Williams, said Joe. Mr. Fields, what were the arrangements made in reference to this murder plot, ask Strickland. Well, the plan was to wait for him to arrive to work in the parking garage where I was going to shoot murder him, "says Joe. "And what happened," asks the attorney pressing for answers. He didn't show up so I called him. Then she arranged a plan for me to call him at home faking that his sister was in a serious car accident and tell him to hurry to the hospital emergency room where I was going to murder him when he got to the parking lot, he says holding his head down not wanting to look at Aaron. "Then as soon as I saw his car and was getting out my rifle the police came to my car with their guns out getting ready to shoot me," Joe says struggling emotionally to recount the incident. Attorney Strickland looks at the jurors and replies. Did Kim at any time during your conversation with her say where she worked," he asks. "She said she works at this place called Remington. She didn't want to talk about her job too much. She was more concerned about making sure I murder him and wanted to get out of the restaurant before somebody notices her. She seemed very nervous," says Joe. For the records please can it be mentioned that the witness identified Kim Downing, the Financial Controller with the Remington Corporation as the person who orchestrated this murder for hire plot," says Strickland. Mr. Fields is there anything else you would like to tell the courts, asks Strickland. Yes, she did say to me that this black man was trying to take over at Remington and she was going to stop it from happening," he says. Pondering his thoughts Attorney Strickland looks up at the ceiling before speaking. "Do you know of any other illegal operations that Kim Downing was involved in related to the Remington Corporation," he asks. "Yes, she hired another friend of mine to cross some telephone wires at the company so she can get information from Mr. Williams' office phone," he said. Attorney Strickland feeling that he has enough evidence to convince the jury of an acquittal turns to the Judge. "Your honor I have no other questions," says Attorney Strickland going back to his seat at the defense table. While the courtroom is stunned at the witness' sharing of information to the court the Judge turns to the Prosecutor. "Counsel, do you want to cross examine the witness at this time," asks the Judge. The Prosecutor hearing the damaging testimony against his case looks in shame as he responds to the Judge's request. "Your honor and members of the jury listening to what we just heard from this witness in specificity and hearing the testimony earlier from the detective of this recent arrest of Joe Fields, the prosecution moves for an acquittal of all charges against the defendant Robert Remington Sr." says Prosecutor Flowers. Alarmed at the Prosecutor's decision the courtroom goes completely quiet. Judge Spalding responding to the surprised move by the prosecution responds in judicial protocol. Based on the prosecution's statements which are recorded and part of the court records there is no need to go further with this trial. As an act of acquittal I find the defendant Robert Remington Sr. not guilty of all charges. I want to say to the jurors, thank you for your time and service. Deputy, you may will you lead the jurors out of the courtroom and Mr. Remington Sr. you are free to go,"" says Judge Spalding before leaving the bench going to his chamber. As Remington and his attorneys leave the crowded courtroom and hallway among well-wishers he is met in the hallway by his wife and children. After congratulatory hugs he and his wife is ushered off to a waiting car avoiding interviews by reporters. As the car slowly pulls off through a busy intersection heading for home Mr. Remington takes a sigh of relief then kisses his wife Sarah.

CHAPTER 18

Two weeks after a very emotional court trial where Robert Remington Sr. was acquitted of all charges and the subsequent arrest of his former Financial Controller Kim Downing he is sitting at home relieved. Knowing that his life has been in turmoil and realizing the damage done to his reputation thoughts of retirement comes across his mind. Conscious of his wife's health with her cancer in remission and his dysfunctional relationship with his son only makes life more difficult. As he is pondering his thoughts in his office den at home Remington hears the alarm goes off signaling that someone is entering his home. "Who is it," shouts Remington making sure he is being heard. "It's me honey. I have Deena and a surprise guest who would like to see you," says Sarah. As Sarah, Deena and Rob Jr. enter into the office den Robert Sr. is shocked by the presence of his son. Before he could say anything negative to his Rob Jr. that will cause a disturbance Deena intervenes. "Dad, we came over to have a talk. Mom and I have had a lengthy discussion with your son and we feel that he is ready to speak freely and respectful of his feelings as it relates to you," says Deena. Can we have a seat dad," asks Deena politely. After acknowledging with a nonverbal gesture that they can be seated Deena looks at Rob Jr. nodding to him to begin sharing his feelings. After a brief pause and sigh in preparation to talk to his dad, Rob Jr. speaks. "Dad, I know that things with you and I have been extremely difficult over the years. I know some of the things that I have done and said in the past were disappointing to you. Because of that I want to openly apologize to you. When you sent me to Harvard University and spent thousands of dollars on my education and when I didn't live up to your expectations you were hurt. I failed you. And when I did finally graduate I was a brooding alcoholic and homeless. Your dream of hiring me as your next successor of the Remington Corporation when you retired went up in smoke. I felt so bad that I was your problem child that I separated myself not just from you but from my whole family. If it wasn't for Deena coming to the city park one day and demanding that I get help for my battle with alcoholism I wouldn't be here today. Then when she told me that mom was battling breast cancer that floored me. For most alcoholics finding very disturbing news, especially about a family member or a love one makes them go deeper into their disease that will eventually kill them. But hearing of mom and realizing my problems it made me look in the mirror at myself. Well dad, what you see in front of you is not only your son, but your son who is in recovery. I just completed a forty two day inpatient treatment for my alcoholism. I know this is only the beginning of my life recovery cycle. I just want to let you know that I will be attending support groups in the future to get my life back in order the way you wanted it to be dad. I came here to openly apologize to you and say I love you. I hope you will accept my apology as I ask forgiveness as I restore the Remington name back into my life," says Rob Jr. as tears start streaming down his face. The room gets extremely quiet except the occasional emotional sounds from Rob Jr. When it seemed as if nothing else was going to be said Robert Sr. responds. "First, thank you for sharing what I know was very difficult for you today. Yes, I was extremely disappointed with you when you failed me. My expectations were so high for you. I sent you to one of the best schools in America to achieve an education. You are right my goal was to have you take over the corporation when I retired. All my dreams for you left when you made me feel that I was wasting my time and money on you. And when I got word that you were an alcoholic and homeless that only push me further away from you. I felt you were disrespecting the family name. Then after all these years of agony between us a change came in my life. That change came when I was arrested and charged with a crime I didn't commit and possibly facing up to one hundred and twenty years in prison. While going through this ordeal I had time to think about the importance of family. I occasionally thought about you. When your mom and sister came and told me that you were in rehab getting help for your disease they call alcoholism I had a different prospective of you. The fact that you went to get help for your sickness was very moving and emotional to me. So much that I instructed my wife to take whatever it cost to find you an apartment and paid the rent for a year until you can get on your feet. In addition, I told Deena to start you a bank account so you would not have to be dependent on others for food and things that you need but no alcohol. And yes son, I forgive you," said Remington Sr. as his son gets out of his chair to give his him a hug. Deena smiles at the positive reception between her dad and brother and responds. "Well this is a cause for a family celebration. Let's go out to dinner and enjoy each other. I will pay for this special occasion," says Deena laughing. As the family prepares to go out the dinner Robert Jr. could see the joy in his mom's face as they were leaving to get in the car.

Three weeks later Mr. Remington Sr. is holding a press conference at the Remington Corporation. Sitting at the end of the large conference room table, Remington Sr. flanked by his board of directors is prepared to make a major announcement regarding changes within the Remington Corporation. With a host of local media and reporters present Mr. Remington adjusts the microphone to speak. "Good morning and welcome to the Remington Corporation. First, I would like to thank all the board of directors who are present. Your service to the corporation has been excellent and one of the reasons why we are a nationally recognized business in the United States. As most of you are aware the last three weeks for me has been very draining for me both emotionally and mentally. After being acquitted of all charges the impact that it has had on me, my family and the corporation as a whole has been very difficult. I would never to myself, my family, my corporation or my community at risk. Today is a very difficult day for me but one that I feel is necessary. On Thursday at a special board meeting I informed the board of trustees of the Remington Corporation that I will be stepping down effective the end of the month from the day to day operations of the Remington Corporation. I just believe that the corporation needs new energy at the top to handle the day to day operations. As a result of my stepping down as President and CEO with the unanimous approval of the board of trustees I have appointed as my successor Mr. Aaron Williams as our new President and CEO. Aaron has shown the ability to lead this corporation to greater heights. Most recently he was responsible for us receiving Fortune 500 status listing as one of the most financially successful businesses in the country by securing a major contract with Cardinal Enterprises. In addition, Mr. Williams has developed a strategic business plan to take the Remington Corporation into the next ten years successfully. Please acknowledge Mr. Williams as our next President/CEO," says Remington Sr. As a round of applause blankets the room Remington makes a surprise announcement. "I have one other very important announcement regarding changes within the corporation. I am also appointing my son Robert Remington Jr., as Mr. Williams' Special Assistant of Operations. He is a graduate of Harvard University earning his bachelors and master degree in Marketing. Over the years he has went through some difficult times where we didn't always see eye to eye. We had a very stormy relationship until recently. But he is qualified to work under Mr. Williams and bring strength as it relates to public relations that are needed under the direction of our President/CEO. Please acknowledge my son Robert Remington Jr., says Remington Sr. Again, a round of applause fills the room as the cameras continue to flicker. As the applause end Mr. Remington prepares to end his session. Before ending this press conference I want to thank my wife being there for e in these difficult times. And I say to you here today. If any of you have a children or family members regardless of their age that you having difficulty with as it pertains to relationships make every effort to make amends with them. It will bring you comfort. What a great time in the Remington family these days. I want to thank God for allowing me to persevere through all I went through. I want to thank my loving wife of forty four years Sarah who never gave up on me. She stood by my side throughout that very emotional court trial, even when things looked difficult. Then we received great news during the trial she is now cancer free after being diagnosed with breast cancer over three years ago. Sarah, I love you and I him to tell you that I will be retiring soon and you will have me all to yourself," he says smiling and getting a laugh from everyone in the audience before turning the microphone off ending the press conference.

Printed in the United States
By Bookmasters